Scattered Crumbs

Scattered Crumbs

A Novel

Muhsin Al-Ramli

Translated by

Yasmeen S. Hanoosh

The University of Arkansas Press
Fayetteville
2003

10 09 08 07 06   5 4 3 2

Designer: John Coghlan

⊗ The paper used in this publication meets the minimum
requirements of the American National Standard for
Permanence of Paper for Printed Library Materials
Z39.48-1984.

Library of Congress Cataloging-in-Publication Data

Raml⁻i, Muhsin.
 [Fat⁻it al-muba'thar. English]
 Scattered crumbs : a novel / Muhsin Al-Ramli ; translated by
Yasmeen S. Hanoosh.
  p. cm.
 ISBN 1-55728-750-3 (pbk.)
 I. Hanoosh, Yasmeen S. II. Title.
 PJ7860.A585 A25 2003
 892.7'37—dc21

2003013599

Acknowledgments

I am grateful to four painstaking and indefatigable readers—Jess Row, Dr. Trevor LeGassick, John Morgan, and Dr. James Cook—for their active encouragement, acute comments and penetrating criticisms during the reading of the final proofs. I thank also Khaled Al-Masri for having given me the idea for this translation, for having introduced me to Muhsin Al-Ramli himself, and for facilitating communications at a time when his own schedule was so thoroughly besieged. To the friendship of all, a considerable debt of gratitude is due.

I am thankful to Scattered Crumbs for having acknowledged some of what the Iraqi people have suffered.

Yasmeen Hanoosh

Scattered Crumbs

To the soul of my brother, Hasan Mitlak,
Because he is some of these scattered . . . crumbs.

They want to convince the people
How wrong they are,
And that the Leader's always right.
Indeed it is a plight.
　　　—Qasim Haddad

Off-Hand

I left my country, retracing Mahmoud's steps, searching for him, dreaming that we might do something and become men worthy of respect so that afterward women—like my cousin Warda, who moved from husband to husband until she ended under Ismael the liar—would search for us.

Mahmoud did not mean anything to anybody, not when he was in the village and not after he left it and the country, slinking away to the North from which no news of him ever reached us. Everyone forgot him completely with the exception of his wretched mother, my aunt. Mahmoud visited her memory at rare and disparate moments, and perhaps she would not have remembered him at all had it not been for the pains of pregnancy and birth and the wiping of his behind with the edges of the crib's sheet when he was a baby. But even these memories of him got muddled in my aunt's mind with those of seven other children who aggrieved her and then vanished. Mahmoud's absence did not mean anything to anybody, just as his presence had not meant anything.

I alone thought of him, and even so I was more curious about what he was doing rather than how he was doing—a curiosity, a longing even, that led me to search for him far from our village. But I have not found him yet. I followed his path and so ended up like him. I slunk away to the North at night with the drunken driver of a truck with broken lights. He sang in Kurdish, as he drove the thundering piece of iron, rising and falling down the winding roads, steering by the moonlight. That was why all his songs were about Layla's moon-face, and that was why I and all the rest of the hitchhikers were wiping the sweat from our brows.

I wondered at the sparkling water of the mountain springs and the waterfalls cascading through the rocks and shrubs that clung to the mountain slopes like children clinging to their mothers' backs. On the peaks the white snow glimmered like silvery hats the size of a dream, so I told myself that this unspoiled paradise was no more than a dream.

The flow of years swept me from one country to another and to the stopovers in between. Nothing strange in this, since stopovers were made for sleeping, waiting, and making transitions. Here I am, a lonely foreigner among foreigners. Telephones are disconnected, letters do not always arrive, and the Spanish newspapers give no news about my family. Did my sister Rubaya recover from her illness? What happened to my cousin who was blockaded in the South? How goes it with our neighbor, whose leg was hacked off in the war? What has become of my friends?

Sad stories become monotonous in Iraq because of their abundance. Each person has trouble that he stopped talking about because his auditors have their own troubles and shut him up with a shrug and a trite "Even the mourner is dead." Then after they shut him up they take to singing Yusuf Umar's song, "The mourner died, Fattuma," which used to get Yusuf Umar jailed under the pretext that "it corrupts public morals." He would excuse himself by saying, "I was drunk. I won't do it again." After three months or so they would release him, and then he would sing it again in the Baghdadi Café, between Abu Nuas Street and the Tigris, where people were drawn to the riverbank by the aroma of barbecued fish. When they locked Yusuf up again, he excused himself again, and people sang the song again whenever you wanted to tell your story. "Forget it, brother. Forget it, man. We want to hear jokes, for even the lantern mender who used to fool around with Fattuma is dead."

Who in Madrid will hear my story when they have no idea what I am talking about, especially when it has nothing to do with soccer, bull fights, or the scandals of movie stars? But I must recall my aunt's face if only to inspire myself to continue the search for Mahmoud, to be able to recognize him if I chance upon him, for he is one of those creatures most apt to be forgotten. I am the only one here who knows about anything there, in my village, lounging upon the Tigris in the site where the first lotus tree took root by accident—they say it used to glow at night and so the evil spirits stole it.

But my village still lies on the riverbank, and Makhoul Mountain still sits on the opposite bank, where the ruins of Assyria's citadel soar above everything. Between them, in the middle of the river, is a small island teeming with jackals, wolves, and nests of black-partridges among the tamarisk trees. There boys sneak over at night to catch the birds sleeping on their eggs but end up catching the lovers sleeping on the sand. They run to tell the village. This is how we know in the morning what happens at night, just as we know at night what happens in the morning.

In the morning we breakfast on the butter from our freckled cow, which my grandfather gave my mother as a wedding gift, mixed with some butter from the village's only Dutch cow, which belongs to my uncle the veterinarian. Each morning mothers meet at the baking ovens, exchange morsels of news, and return to broadcast them to their families, along with the loaves of warm bread and glasses of tea.

—"Amsha said as she hung her wet bedsheet

on the roof of the house, 'My husband peed on me again last night.' Then she repeated his lame excuse, 'Neither doctors nor dervishes did him any good.'"

—"The son of 'Adla the Crippled found the daughter of Corporal Abdul-Rahman with the son of Said al-Attar last night on the island. Sheikh Salih is ordering that they get married to save the honor of our village. And Ibrahim the singer already made up a song about them that he is going to sing at weddings so they buy him off with a goat and its kids."

—"Wadha's donkey untied his tether with his teeth, so in the morning she found him eating the barley from the trough, all the way over at Ghazi's house by the cemetery."

—"Hasiba kicked Qasim in the balls last night, and so today we won't get our radio he was supposed to fix."

During supper—okra, tomato and onion gruel—we learn that the Ajaris quarreled with the Fahads over whose turn it was to use the irrigation ditch for watering the cotton; that Saadi took the young boys to the valley to corrupt them with a jerking-off contest, the reward being the unrestricted use of his behind for one whole evening to do with whatever he pleased; that Ismael prophesied that tomorrow the village would receive the corpses of five of its sons killed in the last offensive on the front; that Farhan is thinking about marrying Aisha—a fourth wife—to renew his bed and that he dyed the hoariness of his head and beard upon hearing of her husband's death in the war; that Halima gave birth to a child she named Abdul-Samad and took him to celebrate his circumcision. And so we learned what was happening every day and what each of us was thinking. People were born in that village, and they died there. What hurt was having the war make some of them die far away.

Doors stay open in the village, and dogs growl only at strangers. Everything has a special name: animals, hills, utensils, rocks, and clouds. For people there are many names. Some are coined after an event and later become famous. Others are given as jokes then persist. Some appear suddenly and disappear when another arrives. Others are given as metaphors and become reality. And there are those to which people get addicted, calling so-and-so the son of such-and-such, or the husband of baker such-and-such, until the real name is forgotten. What is not known today we will know tomorrow, and what cannot be known does not interest us. Then why need we ask about it? Into what part of the apple of life should we bite? What part of the hedgehog are we going to seize?

1

Whether we like it or not, the hedgehog exists. You find him there like the earth itself, rolled up in a ball, his spines sticking out in every direction. Life comes from every direction, so reach out your hand to the hedgehog from any side you like. Your finger may fall on the head or even the mouth. It may fall on the belly or the behind. Or it may not touch the animal at all, like the finger of Ijayel, my aunt's husband, which he drew back when the hedgehog bristled and erupted before him, shooting its variegated needles in every direction, one even into his throat. Ijayel ran home with kangaroo leaps while the lads' airy robes, their *dishdashas,* fluttered around him like the flags that flutter on TV when broadcasting ends and tea glasses fall asleep in their congealed sweetness.

By then Ijayel had not yet married my aunt, nor my father my mother. (Then where was I?) At that time the boys only reached to my grandfather's navel—all the lads in *dishdashas* fluttering around like TV flags. They followed Ijayel home and surrounded him as he stood before his mother forming a fence of bulging eyes that moved closer and grew wider at the moment they realized that the one who was holding his throat could not respond to his mother's questions as she beat her breast in misery. Ijayel's mother is dead now. The last thing she said before her soul slithered out like thread from a hospital wound was, "Nails, nails, nails." Thrice she repeated the word in a subdued voice and then died.

She kept on asking her son what happened to him because she did not know that a hedgehog's needle had been thrust into his throat. He answered her hoarsely, three times, "Bah . . . bah . . . bah," and pointed in the direction of the hedgehog. She asked the fluttering *dishdashas,* but they did not know, for their eyes had not seen a thing.

She lifted with her own the hand that was holding his neck, and then the boys spotted a thin thread of blood waxing and waning whenever Ijayel, who was going to become my aunt's husband, tried to speak: "Bah . . . bah . . . bah." All whose eyes saw the thin thread of blood spurting and receding with the rise and fall of his Adam's apple did not forget his bahbahs, not to this very day when they sit around the coffeepots and discuss the newspaper stories about the European Common Market and the declarations of the American president and cowboy movies and the gory assassinations. Even now they recall that thin thread of blood from Ijayel's throat they saw seventy years ago, and they wonder aloud why Hajji Ijayel is not at the café this morning. They miss the twinkle of his prescription glasses among their own glasses behind which are the now sunken eyes that bulged seventy summers ago, following Ijayel's mother as she led him to his father, who was absorbed in reading the Qur'an beneath the shade of the palm tree on a straw mat made of its fronds, the only palm tree towering in the southern end of the courtyard. He mumbled the formula, "God Almighty speaketh the truth" to conclude the reading, then hastily kissed the book and scurried with his son to the village doctor. The doctor took the wounded boy to the city hospital. The receptionist escorted him to the doctor on call, who was courting the woman doctor on call, so they summarily prescribed eyeglasses for Ijayel, and he returned with his father to the shade of the palm tree. His mother had swept the droppings of sparrows and ringdoves, pigeons and chickens from where they sat. The hedgehog's needle was almost forgotten, whereas Ijayel continued to wear his prescription glasses even on his wedding night, and the bride was my aunt.

She gave birth to Qasim, whose ear a rat nibbled as he slept just after he scratched it upon leaving the dinner table, which had on it a dish of gruel swimming in ghee golden like the sun. My aunt churned the ghee from the milk of her cow, whose death she later mourned. My aunt mourned the cow, and not the cow her, because the cow died first, after the Ministry of Social Welfare sprayed pesticide in order to look after the villages at the beginning of a bygone summer. On that day bands of strange men spread through our village carrying on their backs tanks with long hoses that pumped out drizzle white like milk. But it was not milk because they told us while they sprayed it on the roofs of mud houses that it would kill snakes, rats, mice, hedgehogs, crickets, lice, ticks, worms, spiders, and other things we have since forgotten.

One of the ministry's hirelings was a young Kurd who used the spray to paint a heart pierced by an arrow on the stable walls whenever he sighted an attractive girl. My cousin Warda was more beautiful than the girls in the soap commercial, so for her the Kurd enlarged the heart, then sprayed a long arrow extending from the rooftop, where the sparrows nested among the reeds, all the way to the hut's foundation, with its dung and bucket. He sprayed the arrow in fierce anguish, as he ogled Warda and she stared back at him, and so he forgot to shut off the flow of white liquid until it had already colored the water in the bucket from which my aunt's cow drank. Warda smiled to the painter of the heart and went in to prepare tea. The young man left, and the cow drank from her bucket not thinking about the whiteness of the water. She did not think because she was a cow, and so she died. My aunt cried over the death of the cow from whose milk she used to make delicious ghee for the gruel loved by Qasim, who scratched his ear with greasy fingers before washing his hands and forgot to wash his ear. Then he peed and then he slept, and so the rat came from the hole of its den gnawed in the hidden corner under the deck that held the bed and the mats.

It pleased the rat to come out when everyone slept and to wander through the house, sniffing the damp dirt floor, looking for a grain of rice or a crumb of bread or any remnant of Ijayel's meal. For Ijayel sometimes missed when putting morsels into his mouth, shoving them into his nostrils or his beard instead, because he never changed the prescription glasses he loved so much. They never found that hedgehog, but they used to see the rat. Sometimes in the morning they surprised it in its wanderings, so it would flee to its den. Nobody thought of chasing it further. Nobody thought of tearing apart the deck just to search for a silly rat until they woke up one morning determined to rip out not only the deck, but even the wall supporting the deck and the whole house if that was what it took to get that rat who bit Qasim's ear—one bite after it smelled the grease.

Qasim's ear remained scarred even after he married and became the father of children with many names, some of whom were Ibrahim, Idris, and Shaima, she whose death the doctors are expecting in a few months. Her husband stands beside her bed picturing the village widows in his mind, trying to decide which one is best suited to raise his two children after the death of Shaima, the daughter of Qasim, who managed through his genius in repairing electronic devices, his mastery of the styles of Arabic calligraphy, his inventions and anecdotes, and his intelligence and desertion from the army to distract the people from his ear, to make them forget to ask or laugh about it, or even to look at it.

Despite Qasim's accustomed serenity, he married his sharp-tongued cousin, who could lay waste to a city with her swearwords. He married her because he could not resist the whiteness of her arm that he saw suddenly one sudden dawn when his bladder, bursting with urine, woke him up. He threw off his blanket and trotted outside to the outhouse dug near the baking oven in the corner of the courtyard. He gazed at the dawn around him as he pressed his hands between his thighs and then saw his cousin from behind the low fence as she too trotted to the outhouse pressing her hands between her thighs, gazing at the dawn around her. So they saw each other and she smiled.

That was the first time Qasim saw Hasiba's smile and the first time he saw the naked arm of a woman, and the whiteness of the flesh struck him. That morning Hasiba had gone out in her sleeveless nightgown. Qasim had only seen the faces and fingers of the village women because they were usually bundled up in layers of cloth like onions. He stood with his legs spread over the toilet's mouth, aiming the stream of the urine that gushed out with a mechanical pleasure, and gazed over the wall toward his uncle's outhouse into which Hasiba had disappeared. He thought of her urine and imagined the white flesh and the white arm and her feelings of pleasure and comfort, like his own, upon the release of the pent-up urine. He found himself singing, "Your love reminds me of the Euphrates and Tigris every day. Like the meeting of my soul and yours, pure of heart together they lay." Then and there he decided to unite the sources of their urine whatever the cost. And then and there Hasiba rushed out of the toilet toward the door of the house. Her hair fluttered in the wind, her breasts bounced, her white arm glistened, and she slammed the door behind her.

Was it possible that flesh could be this white, this tender? Qasim remained standing, holding his urine hose as the sun rose while he kept repeating the fatal question to himself: Could flesh be this white? Could what flows under her skin be milk or yogurt or poison and not blood? The questions took him to the riverbank alongside the village. He sat on the pebbles, soaking his feet in the water until night fell. He realized that he had not eaten breakfast or lunch. He had not drawn anything.

He was not aware of the passing of the morning, but it was a morning white like Hasiba's arm whose image he recalled thousands of times along with the flight of her long hair, flowing behind her head like the tail of a beautiful bird. He saw her bouncing breasts in the waves rippling on the strand. He extended his fingers to the bulges in the sand, feeling the tenderness of her breasts and the yielding softness of her white arm. His palm cupped a rounded stone the size of an orange, sensing in it the roundness of Hasiba's shoulder. "Oh, Hasiba, I didn't know that you hoarded this much womanliness behind your man-eater facade!"

He, like everyone else, feared and avoided her if not to dodge the sharpness of her tongue, then to escape the scratching of her wolfish nails or the lashing of the red tamarisk cane she always carried under her arm to take care of her donkey, cows, and those who accosted her. More than anything else, it was the hardness of her foot that led Qasim to stop playing with her in childhood, or so he imagined it to be when he saw it kick the garbage can from under her brother, who had climbed up to reach the sparrows' nest beneath the roof. Qasim knew they were not her sparrows but that she had claimed them nonetheless. He then asserted in his heart, "The sparrows . . . The sparrows are the sparrows of space, the sparrows of Allah."

Her brother fell to the ground, his arm broken and his broken teeth lying in a puddle of blood beneath his face. Paying him no mind, she steadied the can and climbed upon it as Ali screamed, trying to raise himself, the blood spewing from his nostrils whenever he shrieked in pain. Hasiba reached into the nest, pulled out two eggs, and said, "My eggs!" Qasim said in his heart, "They are the eggs of the sparrows, who are the sparrows of space, which is the space of Allah." Then he withdrew in silence. And even though playing with her had been enjoyable, if scary, like playing with a knife or fire, he never played with her again.

Yet how intense grew his longing to play with her when, from the window of his house, he watched her inventing incredible games, lording it over the rest of the youngsters, and bossing them around with all the ferocity of a tigress! But after he saw her kick that can from under Ali with the explosive violence of a bomb, he resolved to play with her no more. He kept avoiding her as they were growing up, growing until his accumulated longing suddenly exploded on that dawn, that dawn white as the whiteness of her arm.

The words astounded him as he heard the Hajji his father asking, on Qasim's behalf, the Hajji his uncle for her hand. For the hand stood for the arm, and how did his father know that he wanted Hasiba's arm and not Hasiba herself? Or that what was important was the arm, and after that came the shoulder, the hair, and only then came Hasiba? This matter boggled his mind. Could his father read his mind so precisely? Did his father possess such perspicacity? Or did he, too, see her arm one dawn? Or did his father perhaps hear him raving about the whiteness of her arm to the river or in his sleep? The bewilderment that inspired such questions continued to roil inside Qasim until after they had been married for some time he divulged it to Hasiba herself and made her burst out laughing. She commented sardonically, "All people say that sort of thing when asking for a girl's engagement, you wise man, you Hasiba's idiot, you silly ass."

It was only when they were alone that she slandered him. When they were with others, she feigned submission and addressed him only as "Abu Shaima," father of Shaima, or "Abu Ibrahim," father of Ibrahim. Qasim himself told me all this after nearly twenty-five years of marriage, so I asked him, "And what is it that kept you stuck on her all these years?" He said, "She's gorgeous, cousin. She's always fiery, always fervent, always fighting, always green, and I am an artist. I love adventures and can't relish life except in those regions dangerous because of their beauty—just as a mountaineer or a bullfighter or a circus acrobat does. The joy of the tightrope walker is the keenest of all, because if his concentration is not present in all his senses and his very being, he falls and dies. Like unto him is the tamer of lions and tigers, for he may be devoured at any moment. Herein lies the true worth of his life, consecrated in an instant. And Hasiba is a restless tigress who makes me live all my years like that one instant, in perpetual flame, on the cusp of continuity and separation, permanence and evanescence. Just like that, forever at a bubbling and boiling moment of truth." He revealed something to me that I and every other village son already knew, that Hasiba feared neither him nor any other person or thing in this world at all—save for her father.

"He's the only one I fear in this world," she would say. "I fear him even more than I fear Allah." For her father, when punishing her, would torture her in ways that became notorious among the clans, and not even their delegations could talk him out of such violence. On the contrary, he would threaten to kill her should the mediators persist. One time he turned her face to Mecca and twisted her arms down behind her, and he stomped on them with his boot. Then he put a knife to her neck and would have slaughtered her like a chicken had not the mediators begged him and fallen on his hand, kissing it, and refusing to leave until he promised not to kill her. Only then did he relent, and then he gave the girl a brutal kick in the head. She rolled over, losing consciousness, while he ordered his terrified, tear-soaked wife to make him strong tea and sat down in the shade on a tin can and smoked a cigarette.

Hasiba was the only sister to seven brothers, all of whom had the nervousness, timidity, terror, and trembling of their mother. Hasiba alone inherited the mad ferocity of their father. When she would scream furiously at her brothers, they could, they swore, see fire blazing from her eyes. Then they would wet their underpants.

2

Long before his seven sons had shot out of my aunt's belly, Hajji Ijayel was known by three characteristics, two of which were unique to him of all creatures in the world. In addition to his prescription glasses, he possessed a singular hoarseness of voice that reminded people of the hedgehog's needle that sank into his throat. Then there was his jingoist obsession that bordered on religion. At least it seemed that way when in a loud, oratorical voice he proclaimed his love of the homeland to the assembly in the village café. He knelt solidly on his knees and his arm shot out of the sleeve of his frock while his fingers impulsively rose in a victory sign.

At the time, everyone was talking about a foreign declaration that called for redefining the borders or something like that. Despite the hoarseness of my uncle's voice, his indignant roar silenced everyone and impelled the sparrows who surrounded him, pecking at the remains of the sunflower seeds that his little boy Saadi was shelling, to fly away in fright.

It is said that he spoke beautifully and powerfully in his oration, or really, improvisation, or even better, "unkneaded" speech, to remind us that he was on his knees as his voice caught fire.

And because he dumbfounded the seated assembly, who could find no way to criticize, belittle, or argue with his terrible words (as they afterwards were described), Mullah Salih, the *muezzin* of the mosque and its Imam, was the only one to take offense at even one of his words, but on account of that one word he rejected the whole speech. At first only a few backed the mullah, and then for fear of Allah, but soon the majority joined him and later so did Ijayel himself. They said to him, "Sit down, man, seek refuge from the devil with Allah. Shame on your hoary head!"

This happened after Ijayel reached the peak of his enthusiasm: after an idea, a radical one, stumbled in his throat and almost choked him because he did not know quite how to say it, so he screamed it instead. Quaking when he finally found the words, he yelled, "I worship my homeland! I worship my homeland!" And before he could repeat them a third time, Mullah Salih interrupted, leaping to his feet and roaring with a fury that drenched his beard with spittle: "Shut up! Shut your mouth! I seek refuge with Allah from you and the homeland you worship!" Then in a calmer tone he reiterated the formulaic invocation: "I seek refuge with Allah. There's no god but Allah. I seek Allah's forgiveness." And he sat down.

Hajji Ijayel's knees shook as he realized the extent of the blunder his tongue had committed, although he still—there, in the bottom of his heart—knew what he had said was truly what he felt, or as close as words could express it. But there was no way to justify what had undeniably slipped from his lips, so he sat, head hanging, fenced in by the same faces and eyes—those of his friends, the lads—that had surrounded him the day the hedgehog's needle lodged in his throat. The voices rumbled in blame and scolding: "Have you become senile, man? You blaspheme! You're over the hill, one leg in this world and the other in the grave!" Mullah Salih moaned. "It's a new heathenism, may Allah be my refuge."

But Ijayel, as everyone knew, had always been enthusiastic for the homeland since his grandfather killed an English officer—"that sonofabitch," as he elaborated whenever he retold the story that took place before the days of the hedgehog's needle and his grandfather's disappearance. His grandfather disappeared from right through independence and until now, and would perhaps will be gone until doomsday or even forever after. He left Ijayel only Three things: a sword hanging in the front wall of the guestroom; an imaginary picture burned into his brain of a dagger piercing the foreign flag and the paunch, stabbing the British Union Jack emblazoned on the belt of the officer sonofabitch; and "nationan," a single word that would stick to Ijayel's heart, tongue, and name forever, for everyone called him "Nationan Ijayel."

Ijayel heard people saying the word to the English soldiers, describing to them his absent grandfather after he had killed their officer sonofabitch; they pronounced the English word "national" with a Bedouin barbarism. And because Ijayel thought, when he heard it for the first time, that it was "nationan" and not "national," he continued to pronounce it like that even after many had corrected him, including his son Qasim.

Qasim tried to learn English in his youth but grew to hate it after he became engrossed in Arabic calligraphy. The aesthetics of this art took him as far as inventing what he called "Qasimicalligraphy." I must say he surprised me with the paintings he showed me, crowded with words in circles and domes, so I asked him to write in the Qasimistyle the epitaph on the grave of my father who, anguishing over the death of one of my cousins and over another missing in action, himself died in the second year of the war.

Now I regret not carrying with me any of Qasim's calligraphy to prove to Mahmoud—when I find him—that I am his cousin and that the only thing that has changed in me is the shaving of my mustache. But I console myself by carrying our password. When we meet and renew our acquaintance, I will say to him, "I wonder if our estrangement is nationan?" And then we will embrace.

Ijayel did not buy a product on which "nationan" was not written or suggested. If he wished to describe a man or a thing that he liked, he would call it nationan. Among these things were my aunt's beans. He used to say, "Her beans are nationan." And although his Aladdin brand kerosene space heater filled his lungs and blackened his face with carbon when its fire flared up while he was asleep, he did not exchange it for another. "Aladdin is nationan." And from among his children he singled out Ahmed, who became a judge, as a nationan son. This was also how he described Abdul-Wahid after his death in the war. As for Qasim and Saadi, "They are not nationan at all because they deserted the army just when the war heated up!"

Two months before his execution in the middle of the village square, Qasim explained his desertion to me as we stood on the bank of the Tigris, in that very spot where he forgot himself one whole day after seeing Hasiba's arm at dawn, or rather the dawning of Hasiba's arm. From what he said, I recall that he rejected the war root and branch because it did not suit his artistic inclinations, because he did not want to kill or be killed, and because war was a farce he did not savor. As for Saadi, as always when asked his opinion about anything from the taste of tea to war or religion, he would say, as do so many, either "This is a nice thing" or "This is not a nice thing." I used to call these "womanish" or "haremish" critiques. And when I wanted to affect preciosity, would add, "The only critical expressions in the *Dictionary of Criteria of Feminine Criticism* are 'Nice' or 'Not nice,' 'I like it' or 'I don't like it.'"

Rather than get upset, Saadi would laugh because he was gay and was aware that everyone, including the government, knew it. "Why do you run away from the army whenever they return you to it, Saadi?" He was silent for a moment and then twisted his neck in effeminate delicacy and with a frozen smile repeated, "I don't like the army and the war is not nice."

Among all of Nationan Ijayel's sons, Abdul-Wahid alone supported the war effort and complied with the orders of the government to the smallest detail. He participated in most of the offensives until he was "martyred fighting for the homeland, dignity, dominion, honor, glory, and soil," as his father would say, parroting the phrases of the TV, the radio, the district police chief, and the village party head.

Death to colonialism! Death to the malicious, spiteful enemy with its yellow wind or yellow smile or yellow intentions or yellow shit . . . or yellow anything! As for Ahmed, since he was a judge, his job saved him from being herded into the war. Mahmoud was young and forgotten. Though he had not reached fighting age back then, Abood, who had but a foggy notion of it all, sang snatches of national songs he picked up in moments of lucidity. Sometimes his mother would thank Allah for making him crazy in her belly, and at other times she would blame Allah for the same thing, and then with tearful eyes hasten to beg forgiveness.

My aunt gave birth to Abood after Warda. He was better looking than Warda, so the village women said, "The honey window opened in your womb. Call him Yusuf." He smiled only one week after his birth, so my mother said to my aunt, "Allah repaid you for Saadi's stupidity with Abood's smile, and for Saadi's ugliness with Abood's beauty." Saadi had been nicknamed

"Abu Angle" because the back of his otherwise eerily rounded head jutted out at an odd angle. Hence the village mayor likened Saadi's skull to the huge rocks used to demarcate plots of land, while others compared it to a tractor battery. Often the thought of strangling Abood crept into Saadi's mind. But once Abood turned three, his family took no more joy in his advent, and pregnant women stopped coming to see him and to cover him with kisses, for ominous changes began to invade him and surprise us.

My aunt was certain that "an envious eye has struck him for his beauty." His blondness gradually turned to grayness. His delicate lips grew thicker and wider until they resembled those of an ape. His forehead protruded conspicuously. His eyelashes lengthened, and his eyebrows turned heavy and black. His nose grew long and pointed until it resembled a beak. By the end of his tenth year he had turned into a fearsome creature with two long arms ending in broad palms and bony fingers, two short legs with wide feet that had difficulty supporting his body, and a gray complexion, in some spots tinted with henna, especially on the back of his shoulders. It was said, in archaic Arabic, that the blending of these two colors resulted in the color *irbid*—dingy gray.

He was not like the other children. If he played with them, they would play tricks on him, or he would lash out at one of them with his long arm until bloodying his victim. Or he would butt someone until his unfortunate playmate's head swelled. He also often banged his head on the wall a lot, on the most solid part of the wall he could find. But his head did not once crack or split, as an onlooker might have imagined. One soon realized that something in this boy's head hurt him, tormented him, something deafening him, like Nimrod's fly. For whenever he banged his head on a wall he scratched it afterwards, focusing on his right temple. "Don't worry," said Nationan Ijayel as he tried to reassure his guests, whose eyes almost burst out of their sockets watching Abood banging against the walls like a stubborn billy goat, "his head is very sturdy!"

It might have been possible to conceal him until the end—whatever that end may be—by simply locking him up in the house had my aunt not insisted on taking her darling Abood out to the fence encircling the yard for some fresh air. But he awoke the village in shock one half-mooned night. Men darted from their sleeping decks and roofs, grabbed their guns, and dashed to Ijayel's house. They surrounded it with gun barrels and cries of alarm. The women wailed and hid behind their doors, with quivering fingers retying the strings of their underwear that had been ravished by the steaming night. They screamed out to their husbands in fear and warning, while the latter busied themselves with the strategy for the upcoming battle. "You, go there; and you, go here; and you, climb up on the roof and have two men stand by the gate. Hajji Ijayel! Abu Qasim! We heard the howl of a wolf from your house!"

"Yes, I heard it too."

Ismael's rebec was audible, moaning along the outskirts of the village, as almost every night. The howl of the wolf rose again, and now they could tell that it came from the direction of the baking oven. Immediately light from their electric torches beamed toward the howl, the oven, that corner. They were appalled—we were appalled—by what we saw: Abood crawling on his arms and one of his knees, raising his other leg like a wolf, stretching to the sky and howling just like a wolf. My aunt left her hiding place behind the door and ran to him. Weeping, she threw herself on him, her heart breaking. "Darling Abood, my baby!" In the strength and anguish of maternity, she pressed his head to her breast. As his mother's odor, which like any noble wolf he never mistook, seeped through to his lungs, Abood's howling softened until he was mewing like a cat, and then he fell silent. Behind the fence the men with the guns eased their grip.

These menacing metamorphoses of Abood, whom she had loved more than any of her other siblings because he had once resembled her like a twin, horrified Warda. She feared the harm they were bringing to him, and also the harm they might augur for her. She would stand at length before the mirror, feeling her tender lips drooping like the strings of sad musical instruments, touching her eyebrows and her breasts with quivering fingers that trembled at the thought that she might undergo a similar transformation. During the day took pains to care for him, giving him the cream of the milk, butter, yogurt, chicken livers, sparrow eggs, and even sugar cane she had peeled with her own teeth. But at night she would be on guard against him. She even slept indoors in the summertime despite the heat, locking the door and the windows, and sometimes covering herself with blankets.

But Warda remained beautiful, as beautiful thank God, as she had ever been and, perhaps due to her bundling up, now even more so. When she awoke in the morning, even before washing, she would leap to the mirror. In front of the looking glass she traced the roundness of her breasts, the fullness of her buttocks, the pomegranates of her back, and the apples of her cheeks. She assured herself of the truth of what her mother had told her when Warda sought her out in the cotton field, collapsed into her lap, and burst into tears: "Oh Warda, my daughter! Don't you see that you've passed the age when Abood changed?" So Warda calmed down, but she began to cry once more, saying, "But he looked exactly like me, mother!" Patiently and with a brave face, my aunt stroked Warda's hair. "But you don't look like him now."

Those who wished to marry Warda or dreamed of her as a lover remained suspended between caution and affection, abstinence and adventure, fear and desire. Meanwhile Warda's anxiety was ebbing away.

She overcame any residual doubt with her mother's reassurance that each creature has its own unique personal destiny and that what was written for Abood on the tablet that Allah keeps was not written for Warda. In short, "Each sheep is hung from its own foot."

Warda's fear of her brother rekindled her sympathy and love for him. Sometimes she took better care of him than her mother did—but only during the day of course, because she was a coward, as she would say of herself, although she knew deep inside that this was not really so. And we realized it too, but it was at least an explanation that relieved one from having to search for the truth.

To this day Warda remains the most beautiful of my girl-cousins, the most beautiful girl in the village. And after I became a high-school student and studied geography, poetry, and history, I would say to her in all honesty, "You are the most beautiful girl in the East, Warda." She would smile, and I would add boldly and enthusiastically, "And even in the whole world!" Then she would blush coyly and withdraw, saying, "I will go make you tea." Warda is many years my senior, so this flirting was no big deal, and my opinion has not changed even today. Whenever a tea party, my aunt's sickness, or a holiday brings us together, I still tell her, "You are the most beautiful girl in the East, and even in the whole world." She remains the most beautiful one, even after her third marriage. And if I return to my country and village again, I will say to her, "You are the most beautiful girl in the East and the West. I've not seen one more beautiful than you in the entire world."

3

Ahmed rushed through the old courtyard gate built by his father's grandfather before he killed the English officer sonofabitch and disappeared until doomsday, a large heavy gate fashioned from oak and cannon nails. Even the worms of the earth gave up gnawing on it, so they merely nibbled a bit before their yellow legions retreated to the neighbors' gate.

He pushed the gate, this time without feeling the heaviness that had fatigued his thin body at every previous homecoming. His happiness made him forget about his body. As he rushed through the gate, he shouted, "Father!" Ijayel, who was sitting under the date palm after the fashion of his ancestors, either reading the Qur'an or reviewing the ladder of grandfathers' names in the family tree, turned to look. How Ijayel wished that his grandfather and father, from whom he inherited this tree, had dug down to its roots and recorded names of such great men as Ashur and Hammurabi, Gilgamesh and Jonah, Noah, Seth, Cain and Adam. Then in the end people might do him more honor than to merely wrap his loincloth around the board that marked his grave.

Ahmed ran to his father, and even before the

boy reached him Ijayel knew from the twinkle in his son's eyes and the sheet of paper he was waving in the air that he had passed his exams again. The Hajji faced a dilemma: how was he going to reward this always good, always passing boy? In the past he had kissed him and stuck a coin in his palm, then patted him on the shoulder and, getting around his inability to find the right words, said, "Go tell the good news to your mother in the kitchen." But this time was different, for Ahmed now matched him in stature, and today's grades were the climax of twelve years of study. Ahmed thrust the paper at his father, shouting, "I am number one in the province!" Ijayel choked in perplexity, not knowing what he should say, just as he had choked before screaming in the village assembly, "I worship my country." He went on staring at the sheet without reading it because he did not need to check the truth of his son's word. He never doubted Ahmed's honesty.

The Hajji gazed at the marks, wondering what praise he could give while the boy stood there snapping his fingers, patient even in his jubilation, until his father lifted his head. Their eyes met in an anxiety of joy bigger than them both. So, as he had done at the end of every other school year, Ahmed offered his cheek to his father, and in this way he rescued Ijayel from his perplexity and from forgetting even to kiss him. The Hajji kissed him with a loud smack like the pop of opening bottles or the smacking of feet in mud. Then he looked again into his son's eyes while looking inward, hoping that he might be inspired with the grandest epithet suitable for this honor. He straightened his prescription glasses, placed his palms on his son's emaciated shoulders, and with tearful eyes said, "You are .. . you are a nationan son, Ahmed!" He lowered his face and saw the list of ancestors' names lying on his lap. He picked it up quickly and said, "This will be yours after me." Then he felt relieved and added, "Go tell the good news to your mother in the kitchen."

Ahmed danced off to the kitchen, and soon trilling cries of joy from Warda and his mother warbled around him. Their words of congratulation echoed loudly, and they could not confine their happiness to the kitchen, so they went out to the courtyard, spreading their ululation in every direction. Neighbors and nephews gathered. Young boys came, and so did old women leaning on their canes. The house was in an uproar, and my aunt scurried to her—very—private box, took out the bag of candy that she had kept since Qasim's wedding, and began to fling its contents into the air above the heads of the crowd. The bystanders scrambled to catch the goodies, and the young boys won the prizes, snatching the sweets from in between the shuffling feet. Kisses rained on Ahmed from toothless mouths. Just before the crowd dispersed at a signal from Ahmed's mother, who had conferred with Ijayel earlier, Abdul-Wahid's voice rose. "Listen, listen. Tomorrow you and whoever else wants to come are invited to an evening feast. We're going to slaughter a ram."

The whistles and shouts of the young grew louder. The old women hailed Abdul-Wahid and Ijayel, who was sitting under the date palm, satisfied with smiling and nodding his head. Then everyone left.

Nationan Ijayel raised his hand to his throat, feeling the scar left by the hedgehog's needle in his Adam's apple. For the first time in his life he felt that this needle, which he had never seen, was dear—as dear to him as the apple, as life itself. He recalled his friends' eyes bulging as they had gathered around him and his mother. It had occurred to him at that moment that perhaps he would die like a camel, without a fight, when on that occasion he heard one of the boys whisper in another's ear, "Is it poisonous?" He had not flinched then, despite the trembling of his heart. He had not asked anyone about it and had not revealed his fear to anybody. And here he was now, a man who had filled his father's house with seven sons, with Warda among them, splendid like the moon.

Ahmed's success surrounded him with cheers and envious eyes. Ijayel imagined that Mullah Salih would hold up Ahmed as an example to his own wayward son and perhaps even overlook the outrageousness of the Hajji's behavior in the assembly when he had declared that he worshipped the homeland because the mullah would now be assured—and I am sure that he was sure—of Ijayel's honesty and his son's nationan success.

Ahmed was always a quiet, ambitious boy absorbed in his solitude and studies. His mother spoiled him by placing a hat with the colored cock feathers on his head. Not all Ijayel's children, however, covered his head with glory, and not all of them were like Ahmed, Warda, or Abdul-Wahid. But . . . that was all right, for even the fingers of one hand are not all alike. Even if his firstborn, Qasim, was an army deserter, everyone respected him for his intelligence and good manners. And people needed him to fix televisions, radios, and refrigerators, or to inscribe placards for shops, banquets, and graves, or to paint the facades of schools and the homes of the rich with lakes, ducks, and boats. For really, he was helpful to people and . . . and . . . to the homeland as well. Ijayel almost did not say the homeland.

After having earlier fought him about it, ridiculed it, and called it "cats' scribbles," Ijayel now thought for the first time to invest in Qasim's artistry. He would send for him, tonight, from his house. And he would ask whoever the messenger is to tell Qasim, "The Hajji is summoning you for an important matter." And while he awaited his son's arrival, he would think of something patriotic to commission him to paint.

Abdul-Wahid, like Ahmed, was also a nationan son. He gave heed to propriety, just like his father. He went to funerals and weddings, visited the sick with his mother, labored in planting the field, and befriended the virtuous among his generation. And it did not hurt that his creeping, premature baldness led him to seek marriage even before Ahmed. Of all Ijayel's children, he was the most committed to the clan's customs and the most obedient to his parents. In all he said and did, the thing he most feared and took into account was what people would say. And if each person in the family, or in the village, had a word or phrase connected to him in one way or another, like his father's "nationan," Saadi's "Abu Angle," Mahmoud's "nothing," Abood's "loco," Warda's "drives men wild," Qasim's "artist," and Ahmed's "scholar," then "shame" was the word most commonly cited in

Abdul-Wahid's dictionary. Of all his siblings, he was the most thin-skinned. As for Saadi's character, Ijayel could find no expression to describe it other than the one his wife screamed in Saadi's face whenever he angered her. "If you hadn't come out of my own belly, I would have said that you're a bastard!" But then Allah's gift of Warda, soul's mercy and heart's flower, warmth of home and life, made up for all her brother's shortcomings.

As for Mahmoud, this boy puzzled everyone because he was so often overlooked, even by himself. Perhaps his father spoke most wisely of him when he said, "He's nothing. This boy is absolutely nothing, a human being with no shadow, at most a number in the census"—as if Mahmoud had no memory, no brain, and no passion. He was very ordinary, even more ordinary than an ordinary person. Sometimes he would disappear, but no one noticed his absence, just as no one noticed his presence. So as not to get sick, he would not raise his voice. He had no likes or dislikes, never got excited or objected to anything, had no distinctive characteristics.

Often the rest of the family simply forgot him. Everyone forgot him, and he forgot himself. He needed no one and no one needed him. He hated nobody and nobody hated him. He did not love anyone and no one loved him. He did not remember people and they did not remember him. You would not think of him except when you saw him, and once out of sight he was truly out of mind.

I do not remember him well, and I cannot come up with a genuine motive for undertaking this quest to find him in a foreign land. Is it because he is the last of his siblings, and if I bring him back to my aunt, she will be happy? Do I want to give him the message Warda entrusted to me when I said good-bye the night before I left the country—"Tell him to become a man worthy of respect"? Is it because I do not know what I ought to be doing in this life, so I claim I am looking for the absent in the unknown when in reality, I do not put serious effort even into that?

I do not want to portray Mahmoud as if he were an illusion, for in the past I have known him in reality, but he strains the memory more than anyone else I have ever known. Perhaps what seduces me is the dream of reconstructing him as I please. Nothing in him is out of the ordinary; and, therefore, nothing of him clings to memory. And if he were not still alive and one of Ijayel's sons who cost my uncle a name and a living and my aunt pregnancy, labor, and nursing, we would not remember him.

My God, how difficult it is to describe him! Indeed he is, as his father said, "a human with no shadow." He is, precisely, "nothing," even after he accompanied the singer Ibrahim, his nephew by his brother Qasim, to the wedding parties in the neighboring villages. My aunt said of him, "He's a creature with no salt." And Warda used to say, "I always forget him when I count my brothers, and when I wash the laundry, the extra pair of socks surprises me, so I pause until I remember him." And, "When I bring the spoons to the dining table, I'm always one short. He rises silently and without irritation goes to the kitchen to fetch a spoon without anyone noticing. Sometimes he stays there to eat, and sometimes he pulls a spoon from his pocket. He never gets angry. He's cold, colder than the backside of the licorice juice vendor."

He was of no importance to anyone. For you, me, her, them, himself, everybody. He was like an anonymous little fish in the darkness of the Pacific Ocean's floor, like . . . Oh, I don't know! He was not even mad like Abood or effeminate like Saadi or social like Abdul-Wahid or smart like Ahmed or artistic like Qasim or beautiful like Warda or patriotic like his father or patient like his mother or harsh like Hasiba or tuneful like Ibrahim or . . . He was a creature with no shadow, a human with no features. He was nothing, nothing, but he was a number in the census nonetheless.

Even Qasim, who painted pictures of many things—the river, the farm, the village, the cows, the donkeys, the chickens, the dogs, the family, the friends—could not find in him anything worth drawing in contrast to Warda, whom he drew seventy times, the last of which was on the afternoon before his execution. There were only two creatures whom he sought to draw but could not, two, no more: his brother Mahmoud and the Leader. Mahmoud because he could not find in him anything to draw and the Leader because he could not bear to draw something toward which he harbored the least hostility. How then could he draw someone he hated with all his heart? That is why his father's unexpected request came as a shock when he sent Warda in the evening to say, "The Hajji summons you for a matter of great importance."

"He wants to try bringing us back to live in the big house again," Hasiba anxiously conjectured. Qasim expected anything but something related to art. After Ijayel closed the door behind them as he usually did when he was about to discuss a serious issue, there came that strange request, to paint a big picture of the Leader! Qasim backed away from his father the length of a surprise, while he gaped at him as if he were seeing him murdered or as if he were seeing him for the first time. Even though the Hajji continued to call Qasim's art "cats' scribbles" and to speak of it with contempt, this was the first time indeed that he—his father—betrayed the least faith in him as a painter and asked him to paint something.

"So! When are you going to finish it? Because I want to hang it here facing toward the guest room entrance." And he walked near the wall, raising his index finger: "Here . . . in front of me."

Qasim swallowed and murmured, "Father, I can't."

Surprise crept into his father's face. "What?"

Qasim hung his head and murmured once more, "Father, I can't."

His father said sharply, "But you painted everything, even Sabi!"*

Qasim did not know how to explain his inability to draw this creature, so he mumbled again, to himself this time, "Father, I cannot."

The Hajji bent close to his face and screamed, "Why?"

"I don't know. I tried doing it more than once and I failed."

---

*Sabi is the name of their donkey. No one remembers how it got its name, but I suggest—to myself—that this name was perhaps given to compensate for their feeling of Mahmoud's (the seventh child's) absence, but I cannot prove this. (Author: Mahmoud's cousin.)

"What's this nonsense? Do you lie to your father's beard, boy?"

"I swear to you."

"Don't swear. You're lying!"

"Believe me, Father, I tried it when I was in the military prison, when I was drawing the prisoners in spite of their crimes or what they had been accused of and when I was drawing the prison mice and dogs and guards as well. But when the warden asked me for that same thing to hang on the prison facade in exchange for improved treatment and help with my pardon, I couldn't, and he didn't believe me, just like you don't now. I couldn't, Father."

Perplexed like his son, both by this revelation and his own anger, Ijayel spun around and screamed at the top of his hoarse voice emerging from beneath the hedgehog's needle, "Qasim, you're . . . You're not your father's son! You're not nationan!"

The door opened, and in came Warda and my aunt to find out what the fuss was about. My aunt held the Hajji to calm him down, while Warda put her arm around Qasim's neck, asking him what had happened. Ijayel vented his indignation at my aunt within hearing distance of Qasim. "Your son Qasim hates the homeland!"

Qasim bent down to kiss his father's palm. "No, Father, don't misjudge me. I love my country, as you love it and as my grandfather loved it. But I hate this man." My aunt asked, "What man?" Her husband answered, "Didn't you hear? He means the Leader. And what's the difference? The Leader is the homeland and the homeland is the Leader."

"No, Father, that's TV talk. As for me, I see the opposite, for the Leader has destroyed the country."

"Coward! Do you call these great victories destruction? You're not a man, and that's why you left your brothers at the battlefront and ran to Hasiba's lap."

"Believe me, I didn't run away out of cowardice, but . . ."

"But you are a sonofabitch, and you don't want the Leader to be a son of the people but an artist and an English sonofabitch like you, or like your disgraceful brother Saadi!"

And Ijayel fell to beating Qasim with his headcord, but my aunt threw herself on her husband's breast, hugging and kissing him. "Calm down, Hajji, I beg you! Take refuge with Allah from the devil. Do you want to beat him now that he's a man with four children?"

Ijayel remained red-faced with a quivering beard, threatening with his headcord, baring his bald head, repeating in furious indignation, "Coward! Traitor! Traitor!" And my aunt begged, "Calm down, Hajji. Sit down. Spare us. The walls have ears."

So she sat him down and signed to Warda to shut the door, but when she went to close it she found Abood crawling on its step. She pulled him in, closed the door, and returned to help her mother, holding her father's other arm and pleading, "Please, Father, don't get mad at Qasim." Abood stretched, stumbling in his crawl, and threw himself into his father's lap, raining kisses on his cheeks, beard, and shoulders as he bleated like a young goat.

My aunt burst out crying, and Warda realized for the first time that that distant being whose

pictures she saw everywhere without paying attention to them had the power to stir up strife between
her father and her brother. She saw this but found
it difficult to fathom, so she also showered kisses
upon the Hajji: "Don't be mad at him, Father."

Abood, who had never kissed anyone before,
managed to calm Ijayel down, for this meta-
morphosed son awakened the pity in his father's
heart if Ijayel was not already secretly feeling pity
for Qasim, his firstborn.

"Alright," the Hajji softened. "Give me some
cold water, Warda."

She hastened in relief, nudging Qasim in the
back as she got up. He took the hint and with a
bow and an apology moved closer to kiss his
father's palm. But Ijayel pulled back his hand,
saying, "Leave me now." Qasim straightened and
pleaded, "I promise, Father, to paint something
that will satisfy you." Then he left.

4

Qasim headed to the Tigris as he usually did
when he wanted to meditate deeply. There he

had once spent a whole day caressing the sand, dreaming of Hasiba's white arm that he saw one white dawn. There also he used to fill in the missing part of his ear with silt and wallow in the ponds. On the strand Qasim had conceived of the Qasimistyle of calligraphy, and on the pebbles he had resolved to desert the army and take no part in the war. There he formed his conviction that it was better to get killed than to kill. And it was there that he talked to me about it all before they executed him in the middle of the village square. And now he went there to think up a painting, a patriotic one to mend what had just gotten torn in his relation with his father.

As he passed the cornfields he saw his brother Saadi, together with a gang of boys, jumping and hopping about among the bamboo stalks. Qasim shouted to him, "What are you doing here?" As usual, Saadi answered, "I'm playing." Qasim bade him go home, but then went on his way without bothering to hear his brother's reply or make sure Saadi followed his order. It would have been useless anyway. Afterwards he was seen in a valley or a field by more than one villager lifting the tail of a donkey to his shoulder, moving his *dishdasha* out of the way, clasping the beast's rear as she mechanically opened and closed her jaws and drooled while the sun of the summer afternoon beat down upon the angle of Saadi's head. He no longer tried to hide his abnormal sexual proclivities. He cared as little about the heat as he did about people's talk. It also made no difference when his brothers beat him and tied him for days to the trunk of the date palm south of the house and his father threatened to kill him. He continued to go out to "play" with the boys in the valleys, woods, and mountain folds, and in the nooks of ruined houses.

When Saadi came to visit us, I would look at him for a long time and compare what I had heard about him to his appearance. He seemed an ordinary person just like other people except for the peculiar angle to the back of his head and his oafish smile. It was hard for me to imagine him doing what people said he did until one July afternoon during our family nap, I found myself in his snare. There was no one there except us, he and I, in the storage room where my father stockpiled things to collect dust "for the future." I was younger than Saadi and playing with him distracted me from sleep and the sun until he took me aback by touching to my testicles. This startled me, and I backed away until I was cornered against the water tank invisible in the dark corner. Meanwhile Saadi's face remained expressionless, a static picture as it were, an oafish smile and dead features.

Slowly he kept moving closer. I wished I could scream to awaken my family or alert our dog that stood panting in the shade. But I was suffocating, and when I considered kicking him and throwing myself on him to beat him away and then flee, I realized that he was a lot bigger than I, for his body blocked out the square of light from the door behind him. He put his hand on my shoulder, which made me start. I brushed it off, for then I remembered that I was in our own house and not his or anywhere else. He whispered to me, "Don't be afraid. I want us to play the chicken and cock game, the bride and groom, the goat and the ram, the dog and the bitch, the donkey and the she-ass. And in this game, as in everything, you'll be the cock and the groom and the ram and the dog and the donkey."

I found myself voicing the confusion that always disturbed me when I heard people gossip about him. "But you're a donkey and I'm a donkey. I mean, you're a boy and I am a boy." "Don't worry," he answered confidently, "I know how to be a she-ass." His voice was thick, wanton, nauseating; and his fetid breath permeated the storehouse. I shook my head, refusing. He brought his mouth near my ear—disgusting!—and said, "If you don't do it, I'll tell my aunt your mother that you want to do me like an ass does a she-ass." Because I did not know what would become of me if my mother heard something like that, or my father or any human being, my scalp froze, and I screamed, "No, no!"

I do not know how, but Saadi somehow read my fear and immediately bent before me, lifting the tail of his *dishdasha* and bunching it under his armpits. So I found myself—for the first time—in front of the naked rear end of a human being. Its enormous size appalled me as it blocked out the world before me. I was looking and not looking, until I heard his voice commanding or begging me from a head I did not see, "Come on! Come on!" He kept swaying as he worked his hands, one there under his dangling head rubbing something in ecstasy and agony, the other spreading open his buttocks before me. Again he shouted, "Come on!" So fearfully I drew nearer and looked at his anus and the hairy blackness around it. I thought of how people hid this spot because of its ugliness, and I found it strange that it did not rot, as it never saw the sun, bundled up there below and inside of them, below and inside all of us, always. Perhaps you could say it was the rotten flesh in us, the source of all our corruption.

Saadi's shaking and gasping grew more vehement as he commanded me in a jagged voice, "Co ..me on .. , .. hu .. rr .. y, .. ev .. en .. if .. wi .. th .. yo .. ur .. fin .. ger!" With this option he saved me from overwhelming horror. I raised my hand hesitantly and extended my middle finger out to the blackness of his rear. My hand was shaking, and my body oozing sweat, and Saadi trembled and screamed, "Come on!" So I hastily stuck my finger into his black darkness and then fled, plunging out of the storage room as fast as I could. I stumbled at the door but managed to reach the carpet of sunlight. I looked at my finger, which I was still holding separate from the rest. When I found it covered to the knuckle with feces, my guts flipped over, and I was overcome by nausea. Thereupon I threw up: Hooooooooaugh!!!!

No one knows how, but later he became one of the top dogs. Anyway, I threw up and on scrubbed my finger with dust and against the wall. Then I crept to the chicken trough and washed it several times. Saadi came out fully dressed in his *dishdasha*, oafish smile, and dead features. He waved to me contentedly and receded into the distance, carrying the wondrous angle of his head.

After that I took pains to avoid him. He, on the other hand, acted as if nothing had happened. He lived his life heedless of people's reactions, even of those who refrained from marrying Warda for fear that their sons would grow to be like their uncle Saadi and that people would joke and wink to one another about them behind their backs. Warda alone was like me— before the storage-room incident. She did not believe what she heard, even refused to let herself hear it. She would get angry when someone tried to tell her these stories.

When Fauzi came forward to ask for her hand, she insisted that he get the approval of her six brothers, including Saadi and Abood, in addition to that of her parents. Fauzi did so, ignoring the disapproval of his own family and friends, as well as the winks of the villagers. He was drawn to Warda's magic and bewitched by the overwhelming images in Indian movies. He had seen them all, from the old black-and-white ones to the modern technicolor ones. At the climax of all these movies, the hero discovers that the one he loves is his sister who had been lost in a flood or in the sewers of New Delhi twenty years earlier. He makes the discovery as he's taking off her wedding gown and sees a tattoo on her shoulder identical to the one he has on his shoulder.

At Warda's wedding people danced outside and trilling cries of joy rose to drown out the boys' screams competing with the celebratory gunfire of Fauzi's cousins. Meanwhile Warda refused to go with her new relatives to the groom's house before speaking to Qasim privately. They all agreed with no explanations demanded, and my aunt closed the door on them after reminding Warda to hurry.

Qasim sat in front of Warda in her wedding dress. She was more beautiful than European Renaissance paintings and the women in the palaces of the Caesars and of kings—a moonbeam in a wedding gown or a creature from a dream—for even her seriousness when she talked did not diminish the power of her captivating beauty.

"Qasim, my dear brother," she said, "how does so distant and strange a man destroy your relationship with your father, and you the light of his eyes?"

Qasim stood up and sighed: "Oh Warda, this isn't the right time for this nonsense."

She rose and placed her white palm on his arm: "I won't go before I know."

Qasim circled around her and spun himself around: "You're crazy, Warda. People are waiting for you outside. Leave this matter for some other time."

"No, now."

"The matter is simply that father believes the TV and thinks that the Leader is developing the homeland, whereas I think the contrary."

"How?"

"Warda!"

"How?"

"Father thinks that the land is more important than the people, and I think the reverse, and the Leader takes advantage of this difference by pitting us against each other without giving a damn about the land or the people. For him, nothing in this world is more important than his throne."

"But he doesn't know either of you. Leave him on his throne and make up with Father. Ever since that evening I've been scared at the way the presence of that distant stranger dominates, though I hadn't even noticed him before. Who is he, Qasim?"

"He's a blood-thirsty creature, Warda, a vampire; that is, a monster. He will slay us if another man does not rescue us from him."

"What other man, Qasim?"

"I don't know, but surely he'll be . . . a man worthy of respect."

"Do you think Fauzi is a man worthy of respect?"

"Oh, Warda, leave off now! People outside are waiting for you. We'll talk later."

Warda gazed deeply into her brother's eyes until he leaned forward and kissed her forehead, saying, "Congratulations." Her eyes filled with tears, and the wedding blazed outside. Then Qasim hurried out, passing under the bullets fired in celebration, to the haven of his Tigris shore to contemplate painting a picture, a patriotic one, for his father and for Warda.

5

Even after he reached the twinkling ripples of the river, the gunshots still reverberated in his ears. "Even the face of our joy is warlike and armed," he said to himself. Then he squatted, scooped up some water, and sprinkled it on his face, ears, and neck in the hope that the bite of its coldness might take away his anxiety. He moved to a nearby rock, sat on it, and dangled his legs in the water, gazing at the face of the river and glancing occasionally at the green island in its middle. He had to get to the root of the problem. If he wanted pure sand, he could plunge his arm into the river up to the elbow and grasp a handful of the bottom, then lift it to see clean washed sand between his fingers. He also had to do this in his meditation: thrust his focus down into the beginning when the Leader casually declared war before his parliament, whom he already knew would ratify his declaration because he, not the people, had chosen its members. And it did not occur to anyone who knew the situation—and everyone knew the situation—that a rural deputy who could barely read or write would dissent.

The surprise of the Leader equaled that of the whole world when he saw a hand rising to object. The rural representative said—within earshot of the guards and the other representatives but not the TV microphones—that a border dispute with neighbors did not necessarily mean war, otherwise all the countries of the globe would be at war. "Sometimes my neighbors and I raise the wall between us and lower it at others. At times we plant its top with glass shards and with flowers at others. But we have not slaughtered each other because neighbors are family, and all warfare is despicable, and even the winner is a loser."

Perhaps he did not say that exactly, but that is the paraphrase people passed around and hoped was said. And it must have been something like that. No smoke without fire, as the proverb of the old folk says.

It was said that the Leader welcomed the representative's opinion. He was democratic, and so he invited the rural deputy to confer with him privately. He took him to a side room in the conference hall—it could have been the bathroom. Then from behind its door, the gentlemen of the assembly heard a muffled pistol shot, after which the Leader came out inquiring about other dissenting opinions. He did not find any, so he declared the war in the name of the people and its representatives, and the war took to its trenches Qasim and Abdul-Wahid and Saadi and Jaafar and Samit and Faris and Fauzi and Ali and Ghazi and Abed and Khdayir and Muhammad and Kathim and Hussein and Omar and Amin and the date palms and the oil and the schools.

We heard of victories and the raising of flags over liberated lands that expanded the way our village cemetery did, with the aid of the corpses of our village sons. They were wrapped up in the flags of the homeland, and other flags fluttered above the graves until our old cemetery was transformed into a forest of flags of homeland under which mothers still weep every Thursday. The TV kept on repeating the *Khansa Show*— about that poetess of old who took great pride in the warrior martyrdom of her father, two husbands, two brothers, and four sons—six times a day, before and after meals. When Qasim deserted from the front, Saadi followed him, saying, "It's not nice." Then Ismael followed them with more than one lame excuse. The TV started raining thousands of cowboy movies on us, for manliness and killing come easier than slipping on banana peels.

When the war dragged on for years and some of the old men complained around the coffee-pots about the inability of departing shoulders to carry family burdens, Hajji Ijayel kept on repeating in their ears all the declarations of the Leader and all the benefits of the war. He reminded them of the sweetness of victory that would surely come after a prolonged struggle—no matter how prolonged!

The government added other TV channels specifically for broadcasting cowboy movies, the *Khansa Show*, and the series on the Besus War, a soap opera version of the ancient tribal conflict whose broadcast was interspersed with images of the Leader. The Leader bestowed upon each of us citizens a TV set that worked on solar energy should the electricity fail. And we, the students, donated our blood to the wounded, while women donated their gold for the purchase of arms and the making of medals for the valiant and gold statues of the Leader. The old men volunteered to fight. At the head of their pro-war demonstrations, arranged by the Party, stood Hajji Ijayel. The leadership thanked them and agreed—after the old men insisted and raised our forefathers' swords and banners—to take the able-bodied among them into the army reserve. The poets swore by the life of the Leader, and then by Allah, that victory was ours, however long the war might last. The singers' throats crooned tunes that praised the muscles of the Leader and the greatness of his mustache, symbolic of the scales of justice, as well as his blood, inherited from the Prophet, and his unique genius. For he was inspired, omniscient, and full of a wisdom that ranged from the doctrine of the people's need for the toothbrush and an enormous tome on the advantages of toilets, and on and on to spaceships and promise to liberate all the lands pillaged by imperialism wherever they might be, even on Mars or the moon, because we were the first in the world to discover the moon, the proof for which was the poetry of Ibn al-Mulawwah on Layla al-Amiriyya—those poems whose eloquence was unsurpassed save by the words of the Leader himself when he said, "The land needs blood the way women need to paint their lips red." Afterwards they wrote his proclamation in gold and blood.

A fish bit your big toe, Qasim, so you jumped and screamed in red, "I got it!" When you found the homeland covered in red and the world of blonde women around it green and your heart green and the homeland in your heart, you ran and ran and ran to the village, to your home, to the painting room—not stopping to eat any of Hasiba's food—and you painted on the largest canvas you had a map of the homeland in red. You circled it with a large green heart. Then you drew the two rivers in white. You were trembling with love as you swayed down with the meandering lines of the two rivers surging from north to south. Then when they met in the waterway of slaughter, you wept. You cried until you almost fainted, and fell prostrate before the picture as you watched through your tears how the white pigment ran over the canvas like water, or even tears. Why these two rivers in particular? You wished to name them, to describe their embrace, or to describe that feeling which shook you as you drew them—shook you as you gazed at them and struck you with love and agony when they met, as if they had passed through all the regions of your body and then united in the deepest fold of your heart. "Your love reminds me of the Euphrates and Tigris every day. Like the meeting of my soul and yours, pure of heart together they lay."

Hasiba came to call him to dinner, and her mouth gaped open when she saw him lying on the ground stained in red, green, and white as if he were wrapped in a flag like those who returned from the war in the victory coffins. She gasped and ran to lift him under his armpits and stand him up, and then she embraced him in his paint and wept on his shoulder at the edges of the spattered white. Qasim drew her to his chest in the certainty that he would love her forever. He imagined her tears flowing with his body on her whiteness, or with the whiteness on his body, and descending to the south to meet at the foot of the homeland, or at his heart. All of it was homeland.

He carried the canvas in his arms and flew to

his father in rapture. He pushed the aged gate without feeling its heaviness, embroidered with cannon nails as it was. He waved the painting, exactly as Ahmed had waved his grade report, to his father, who was sitting under the date palm, so the Hajji raised his prescription glasses. The saliva he swallowed finally passed beyond the hedgehog's needle. He smiled to Qasim, or to the homeland in the heart, or to the two rivers in the homeland in the heart, and led him to the guest room to hang it there in the front—so he desired—in front of him and in front of them. They stood before it and behind them, all in a row, my aunt followed by Ahmed, Saadi, Mahmoud, and Abood. Qasim did not feel the silence, nor did he feel the time passing as they stood there, for he was overflowing with joy as he moved his gaze back and forth between the homeland map and his father's face. But then he became worried by the furrowed brow, the pursed lips, and the rise without descent of the Hajji's Adam's apple, until the Hajji said, "Exactly, Qasim. This is a nationan picture, but . . ." My aunt raised her hand to her chest in apprehension. The son's eyes gazed at his father's white beard until after a moment Ijayel added, "But you reversed the colors." Then he hesitated before relieving their suspense altogether by completing his statement. "You should have made the homeland green and the heart red, as they are in truth and reality."

With labored breath Qasim almost replied, but with difficulty managed to repress his desire to explain, because that would mean saying that he saw "truth and reality" opposite to the way his father saw them, so he resorted to a different answer: "Pardon me, Father, but according to my knowledge of painting and the proper use of colors, I found that if I had painted this picture in any other way, its balance would have been wrecked." Then he added, "The principals of art require . . . that." To himself he meant "honesty," but the necessities of the situation forced him to change it to "that." The father patted his son's shoulder and said, "What matters is that it's the homeland's picture." So Qasim repeated after him in a low voice with a sigh, "Yes, it is the homeland's picture."

6

The summer grew hotter and the war more voracious. It brought convoys of flags, medals of honor, and village youths in coffins back to us. To make good on these losses, the police launched a big campaign to arrest all deserters, so they took Qasim, Saadi, Ismael, Kamil, Nuri, and Seth and threw them behind the military prison's bars, in long halls of cells that used to be stables for the English horses before independence. Until public attention induced the authorities to put them in solitary confinement, each hall featured one of Hajji Ijayel's sons as its main attraction.

While Qasim gathered around him the prisoners of his hall to draw them in varied poses and to tattoo their arms, shoulders, and chests with phrases of love, freedom, and torment, Saadi's prisoners selected their finest sheets to put under him in an attempt to regain some of the warmth of their wives' beds at night. The guards were the first to get drawn or tattooed by Qasim and the first to lay Saadi on their sheets.

When news reached the warden, he ordered Qasim to paint a picture of the Leader, and when he could not, he was placed in solitary. The warden ordered Saadi to stop keeping the prisoners up at night, and when he failed to comply, he was isolated as well. But Saadi took off his underwear and climbed up on the shit canister in his cell, placing his behind in the little window that separated him from the rest of the prisoners in his hall so that they in their turn could climb up and get him from there. When the warden learned of this, he became infuriated and transferred Saadi to a private chamber next to his office, where he was provided with all the amenities reserved for prominent prisoners.

Later on it was said that there had been a narrow secret passage connecting the office with Saadi's chamber, covered on the office side with a file cabinet and on Saadi's with a closet for undergarments, including brassieres, and red nightgowns. Saadi never denied these rumors, nor did he bother to comment on them with more than an oafish smile, frozen features, and repetition of the sentence, "Yeah, those were nice days with Mr. Warden!" Qasim likewise did not bother to add that without Saadi it would not have satisfied Mr. Warden merely to isolate him. He would have tortured Qasim to death.

The war intensified, so the Leader pardoned all military prisoners and returned them to their units. He also released all political prisoners from life and returned them to the belly of their mother earth after they had impregnated the refrigerators for a period long enough for their parents to pay the cost of nooses, the importation of which would have cost the government hard cash.

On leave after the pardon, Saadi asked his mother to weave him a shoulder braid to put around his shoulder like a corporal. She did so with joy, thinking that he had been promoted and was going to continue his military service. However, that did not happen. After more than one successful attempt to fake a higher rank, even that of an officer, Saadi got bored with the military life because "It is not nice." He fled to the cornfields where boys, donkeys, and pleasure lay. Qasim escaped also after he saw ravaged cities and villages and entered houses whose owners had fled, leaving tea glasses half-full, pictures staring in bitterness, and wedding clothes in the closet. He was able to make it to the wedding of his daughter Shaima, that delicate, thin girl, submissive unlike her mother. His joy at her wedding was a genuine joy such as he had not felt since his own wedding with Hasiba, who feared that illness might assail her daughter before the wedding, and so she could not keep from dancing as she beheld her daughter in the white wedding dress. The girl looked small, beautiful, like a child's doll, her fingers clinging to the elbow of her fat groom, whose blubber almost rent the sleeves of his suit and burst its buttons as he wiped off the sweat oozing from his flushed temples and squat neck.

The heat was intense and so was the war, so the government formed a committee of squat-necked and choleric experts to reassess the physical, psychological, and mental criteria by which a citizen was judged to be exempt from military service or flung into it. The committee was also to reexamine all the homeland's precious lunatics, including Abood al-Ramli, whom the police put in their car after they wrestled him out of my weeping aunt's lap as she begged them, "I swear by Allah, the boy is crazed, the poor thing." Hajji Ijayel tried to calm her down by saying, "They're only doing a simple test, and then they'll return him," although deep inside he wished they would take him into the army because the army was the maker of men. He hoped that it might remedy his son's condition so he could fill the gap left by Saadi and Qasim. On the way he told the police the story of Abood's life from the time that he was born a beautiful, laughing boy. He also told them, proudly, the story of his grandfather who stabbed the English officer sonofabitch, and he told them that he had another son called Ahmed who was first in his university in studying law and so the government was going to appoint him as a judge, and that he had another son called Abdul-Wahid at the front line. But he did not say a word about Saadi, Qasim, or Mahmoud.

As he stood before the committee after waiting in line with thousands of misfits, holding the sun-stroked Abood up by his collar, Ijayel repeated what he had told the police. One expert with a big bald head barked at Abood, "What's your name?" This startled Abood and made him tongue-tied. His father repeated the request to him, reminding him of the names he had learned under the date palm, so Abood recited the names up to the tenth grandfather until the bald man said to him, "Count for us from one to ten." Relishing the memory of the rhyming game that Saadi and the village boys had taught him, Abood began counting to the bald man, smiling and humming the forced end rhymes. "One, you'll mount someone. Two, I'll ram it in you. Three, you're screwed by Uncle Ali. Four, your ass is sore. Five, your father will drive. Six, we have longer dicks . . ." He ignored the shouts of his father, who set about trying to stop him. "That's shameful, boy! Boy, shut up!" Hajji Ijayel tried to remind his son of the verses he had taught him from the national anthem, but he could not stop him. "Seven, I'll ride you to heaven. Eight, your cock's a dry date. Nine, your balls are smaller than mine. Ten, I'll mount sissy men." Then he jumped up and down, clapping elatedly as he used to do when playing that game with Saadi and his friends.

The committee did not buy this show of idiocy, nor that of thousands who performed better scenes of hysteria and lunacy in the hope of saving their skin. Although the officials duly noted the strange thickness of Abood's eyebrows, the protrusion of his forehead, his beaky chin, and dingy color, they nevertheless transferred him, like the rest, to the torture room—"the Sieve"—in which the strongest of charlatans weakened under the sting of the thick electrical cord.

Abood giggled at the fall of the first few lashes upon his skin while his father averted his eyes in pain. After a few minutes the screams rose until they shook everyone. Abood let out a wild, wolfish howl, so perfectly wolfish that it frightened the flogger himself. The committee was thus assured of his insanity and dumped him with his father on the sidewalk, where Ijayel sought help from some good Samaritans to lift

Abood onto a sack in the trunk of a taxi that took them back to my aunt, who was sitting in front of the oakwood gate waiting for them under the sun.

But to her surprise, when she stood up and stepped forward, opening her arms to receive Abood, whom the driver and Ijayel had dragged from the trunk by his armpits, she instead received Warda, who ran into her mother's arms silent, listless, haggard, parched-mouthed, and with disheveled hair. Ijayel left his son in the hands of the driver and rushed to Warda, questioning her. She gasped, then burst out crying on my aunt's chest, "Fauzi died, Mama." My aunt screamed, "Yibooooooooo! Miserable Um Qasim!" For a moment the Hajji stood as if pinned to the ground, then turned to the driver and said, "My son-in-law was martyred in the war fighting for the homeland."

Although Warda gave Fauzi a daughter as beautiful as herself and insisted on naming her Warda before leaving the baby with Fauzi's parents, she had not been able to decide during the entire period of her marriage whether or not

Fauzi was a man worthy of respect. She strove to find the answer in light of what Qasim had said about the man who deserves respect. This uncertainty is what hurt her the most in her husband's death. Perhaps he was a man worthy of respect, but his monthly seven-day leave was not enough time for her to find out. The war had more of him than she, until it took him forever.

7

Fauzi and Abdul-Wahid fell in the same battle, but Fauzi, wrapped up in the flag and accompanied with the badge of honor, arrived home before Abdul-Wahid, wrapped up in the flag and accompanied by the badge of honor both of which the party leader and police chief deposited into Ijayel's hands with all due respect and courtesy. The former said, "Congratulations on the martyrdom of your son." The latter added, "He was a valiant hero who watered the soil of the precious homeland with his noble blood."

My aunt smeared her face with soot, poured the oven's ashes on her head, and sagged to the ground like a slaughtered ewe. Ijayel tried to remind her of the *Khansa Show*, but her memory had fluttered away. The screams of women rose in a funereal dirge that filled the courtyard. The elderly women wailed in old verse:

> May life get no longer,
> > May it get shorter still.
> End our wretchedness yonder,
> > Sigh upon sigh will kill.

Abood did not understand a thing, so he howled. Mullah Salih patted Ijayel's shoulder as if rebuking him: "Say, we come from the hand of Allah and to him we shall return." Ijayel echoed his words, and then added, "Did you see, Mullah? Abdul-Wahid is a nationan son." The mullah cast a puzzled look at him and then moved away, whispering, "May Allah forgive you." Qasim wept bitterly and said to the riverbank, "They've shed your blood, son of my mother, for no reason. My God, how painful that is!" Saadi kicked at the bamboo stalks and smacked them against each other, screaming, "Stupid, dumb idiot! Abdul-Wahid is an idiot!"

Then he cried and slept in the fields for days. Warda scratched her cheeks, tore her dress, wore black, and wished she could howl like Abood, but her screams at the loss of the two made her lose her voice for a long time. In time she married Aqiel, and then asked him to divorce her after she left him a daughter as beautiful as herself, whom she also insisted on naming Warda.

Aqiel tried to talk her out of divorce but she would not bend, so he gave in because she could no longer stand living with him after she discovered that he was a man unworthy of respect. She realized this when she demanded that he define his position with regard to that distant stranger. He said, "Whoever marries our mother becomes our father, so leave us in peace!" So she cast her peace upon him and went out, returning to her parents' house, determined next time not to marry anyone but a man worthy of respect. She looked for this man even in the city when she traveled to attend the wedding of Ahmed, who married a city "foreigner" as my aunt, who had been hurt by his departure, branded her daughter-in-law. Ahmed settled there, occupied with his career, wife, and children, who were thus deprived of their granny's upbringing. The oldest of them was a child of sharp wit. He beat everyone in chess, including his father, grandfather, and Uncle Qasim, so my aunt gave him his father's old hat adorned with a pied cock feather that she had kept along with the strap of Ahmed's cradle in her shabby wedding box. Qasim painted a nice picture of his nephew playing chess. His grandfather told him about his Uncle Abdul-Wahid, the "hero," and about his grandfather who had killed the English officer sonofabitch.

Ijayel continued to boast about his two heroes, mentioning them wherever he went—to the assembly in the village café, on the road to any driver or passenger he chanced to meet, to the worshippers in the mosque after Friday prayer, and at home to the neighbors, his guests, Abood, and the courtyard's date palm. Qasim, on the other hand, cried out to the river bitterly, "Alas!"

Gray invaded Qasim's head, and his face grew grimmer. Thus Hasiba and the boys were surprised when one day—as he heard the Leader on TV issuing a decree for cutting an ear off army deserters—Qasim burst into a fit of laughter so fierce that he flipped on his back and his thighs were bared as he kicked in the air with his feet.

Hasiba went to him and sat him up as she pulled his *dishdasha* down to cover his thighs from the boys, asking what was so amusing. He put his hand on his nibbled ear and said through his guffaws, "The rat bit one half of it, and he'll bite the other half." When word got round, the village roared with laughter, and irony heated up among the people. It was asked, "And what if one deserts a second time?" And the answer came, "They'll cut off the other ear." It was asked, "What if one deserts a third time?" This brought forth a number of replies, and one wit earned a hanging for conceiving it: "He'll cut off *that* which Saadi loves." And he who followed this joker to his death quipped, "So he's going to compete with that boy in earning his bread." Since people were so amused to imagine themselves with chopped off ears, the Leader amended his decree to one of execution.

Swarms of police now chased after deserters. Saadi hurriedly hid before they could take him unawares at the oak gate. They searched everywhere—in the bedrooms, under the beds, behind the doors, in the kitchen, on the threshing floor, in the water tank, on the roof. They peered into the well as Warda stared at them with hate and then spat on the ground until they left. Then Saadi crept out of his lair under the she-donkey, who was draped in a long rug that hung to the ground. He stroked her neck and fondled her ears, promising to treat her better, and then strolled to the kitchen.

Meanwhile they caught Qasim when they broke into his house and found him in the painting room, absorbed in his colors. With all the strength of her voice, Hasiba gave a cry that reached the entire village and even the farmers in the nearby fields. We all ran toward the screaming and arrived in time to see a police officer putting Qasim's hands in iron behind his back and leading him to the middle of the village square. We walked behind them, men entreating policemen they knew and women imploring any policeman who would listen. A warm, nightmarish afternoon, whose calamity everyone had foreseen, enveloped the village. The police ordered Hasiba to stay at home. She raged against them, and they found that only her father could persuade her to keep to the house with her sons. Hajji Ijayel went into the guest-room and shut the door. After they closed the door and the windows and covered them with blankets to admit no sound, Warda threw herself on my aunt so they could cry. The noise of the road pebbles under the boots of our marching troops was like the scratching of skin with rough claws. Dust flared up from their feet and turned into mud on their faces, clinging to the sweat that poured forth in heat and bewilderment, impotence, and fear. We were like a flock of cattle, and cattle are cattle, whether silent or strident. There is no difference.

They stood Qasim in the middle of the courtyard and pushed back the throng that half-circled him. Mutterings of sorrow or pain, whispers of protest that would not be heard, pious mumblings of "No strength or power but by

Allah," and pleas and labored breathing collided with words that shot from the mouth of a policeman: "A decree!"

A white sun glaring, women weeping, old men trembling, children shrieking, date palms wilting, sparrows flying, and Qasim's head and disheveled hair drooping. They shackled his feet, and his hands behind his back. His clothes were stained with the colors red, green, white. And memories of him hovered in the heads that surrounded him.

He had painted shop fronts, fixed radios, and inscribed grave markers for them. He had prepared own grave marker a long time ago at the beginning of the war and set it in the corner of his painting room with a few old paintings: "Here lies the human being, Qasim Ijayel al-Ramli, with his dreams. He is the founder of the Qasimicalligraphy. He was deadened but not dead." On the back of the marker he wrote Tagore's saying, "I bow before you all, then proceed on my journey."

Colors. Colors and frowns and confusion and dry impossible commotion. Yellow faces, pounding pounded hearts, voice boxes that lost their voices, throats that quit swallowing, parched, surfeited with the taste of desert sand and the smell of blood, salt, tears—or no tears. Eyes that looked and did not see. The police chief asked Qasim what his last wish was. The half-circle of people moved nearer but would not have heard had not the officer screamed at one of the policemen, "Go fetch him his father!"

Qasim wanted to clarify many matters to his father, or to cast a final look at his dear glasses and ask his forgiveness for a flood of coming sorrows, or to hint that there was no difference between his own death and Abdul-Wahid's, for the killer was one and the motive was one, and the police chief who bestowed upon him Abdul-Wahid's badge of honor would also take from him the cost of the bullets used to execute Qasim and write on Qasim's coffin, "Traitor." He wanted to embrace his father and look into his eyeglasses in the hope that his father might understand his son and carry to Hasiba and his mother and Warda the meaning of the last light faltering in his eyes. To tell them that he did not want to depart but that they had forced it upon him, or to transmit to his father, to all of them, to all of us through his father that after death he would become like him, like all of them, like all of us—bereft of volition and freedom and the dream—and his head drooped in sorrow over him, over all of them, over all of us, and over the beauty of the Qasimicalligraphy and the riverbank and life. He was—like their heads, like our heads around him—swayed by the swinging of all eyes between his head and the anticipation of the emergence of his father's head, which never emerged, for the policeman returned and said, "He refuses

Pain wrung Qasim in a painful moment, more painful than bygone pains or pains yet to come. The officer drew near and the ears around him strained to hear. "Then don't waste our time. Ask for something else, quickly!" Qasim raised his head, and the villagers watched, and the world watched them, and he wished to say, "I want to see the Tigris River. Kill me there where I have been going since childhood, where I still can see Hasiba's white arm in the white dawn, the red homeland in the green heart, the rock and the fish, the Qasimicalligraphy and the sand, the decision not to join in the murder party, the island in the middle of the river, pebbles, shore, seagulls . . . seagulls and waves, and the drift of water is long, it takes long . . ."

The officer stared as his silence took long. He repeated to him impatiently, "What do you want?" Qasim shook his head. "Nothing."

The police chief signaled to the guards to blindfold him, and at a sharp command the police officers stood before him in a row. Then, as one, they knelt upon the ground and aimed the muzzles of their rifles at him. Women screamed in horror, and some of them fainted. Children ran away and old men looked into the clouds. Palms covered their eyes so that they would not witness, or so that they might see from between their fingers. Some averted their faces. The officer shouted, "Fire!" The guns roared, and Qasim fell to the ground under a crazy leaden rain that perforated his body with red holes that looked like red anemones.

Behind the door Hasiba and her boys heard

the rifles explode. She screamed like a wounded lioness. Her upright father sat down. Behind the door, Hajji Ijayel seized his throat, his Adam's apple, his hedgehog's needle, and felt it hurt him for the first time in his life, as if the bullets were piercing it. Behind the door Warda closed her mother's ears with her fingers, so she heard the first shot and then ceased to hear. But who was there to close Warda's ears?

Red holes, and then red gushed from them, and he collapsed in red. We and the sun stared at him, huddled on the red ground. A blink of an eye. Qasim writhed a little in a final, feeble movement, as if trying to lift his body, then dropped . . . A corpse forever.

8

Absence. Or the other face of presence. Perhaps its flip side. Qasim, his soul, was absent from life, even if his corpse remained in the village square guarded by two policemen and flashes of him obsessed some, Warda and Hasiba above all. Abdul-Wahid was absent in the cemetery,

Ahmed was absent in the city, and where Saadi was, absent no one at first knew, but some who came from the capital said they saw him there. They saw him in bars and restaurants and hotels, laughing with the relatives of the Leader. They laughed, and he traded their old cars for them. It was said that he worked for them, and in return they supplied him with perks and favors. It was said that he had become rich and covered the protruding angle of his head with the headcord and *kaffiyya* that Ijayel had not put on his own head since Qasim's execution. Ijayel absented himself from the café assembly, and from people in general, secluding himself in the corner of the guestroom, supine, staring at Qasim's painting.

A red homeland, a green heart, and two white rivers. He stopped talking about the heroism of his grandfather, or Abdul-Wahid's. He stopped talking altogether, except for signs to request water or help to the toilet. My aunt sat next to him, haggard, with eyes ever shedding tears, wrinkles etched on her face, eyelids, and hands. She and Warda took turns swabbing the thread of blood that descended from Ijayel's

Adam's apple, the thread that had reappeared, after more than seventy years, at the instant he heard the first bullet enter Qasim's body. Ijayel felt the pain of his hedgehog's needle as he had never felt it before, for it had not hurt him like this even at the moment it penetrated his neck in that game long-ago among the boys in their *dishdashas* before his prescription glasses.

The thread of blood refused to go away. Whenever Warda or my aunt wiped it off, the needle bled another thread immediately. When he noticed fatigue and despair overcoming them, Ijayel would stop their hands from wiping it. His pain intensified whenever he gazed long at the painting in which he saw Qasim's face sometimes, the face of his first son, the son whose coming into the world assured him that his masculinity was intact. Qasim's death in this dreadful fashion put his father at a junction of sharp edges: between Qasim and Abdul-Wahid, which one was . . . ? Questions, questions, and he did not know what to say. Answers did not come so easily to his pierced throat as used to be the case. Both of them were blood of his blood. He stared again at the red map that had taken both of them and at the manner of their taking. The answer was just: it took them. Because he did not understand, his eyes overflowed with tears and the blood trickled down his Adam's apple. My aunt wiped it away and cried as she saw two tears glide down the sides of the Hajji's face. She began to complain to him about her state, and Qasim's state after his execution. But Warda glared and bit her lower lip, silently warning her mother to leave Ijayel, alone of all people, without the knowledge that his son's body had been left in the middle of the square for three days.

The two policemen said, "The government wants to make an example of him." We, the beneficiaries of this example, passed by a slight distance from him, saw him red, twisted and huddled in the brook of his blood that had coagulated and then dried, sticking to him while blue flies buzzed around his bullet holes, rising and falling and entering them. The two policemen did not shoo them away—they barely shooed a dog that sniffed at him—nor did they discourage the curiosity of the people until on the afternoon of the third day Mullah Salih took them aback when, without the permission of the two policemen standing in the shade, he took off his cloak and covered the body with it.

They immediately grabbed him under the armpits and dragged him away, imprisoning him for six months, after which he returned sickly, shaking, and sallow and dedicated Friday sermons to prayers for the congregation's long life and for victories so that those might prosper who found in Saadi a tool who did not care and in Ahmed a fragility more stubborn than the sturdiness of their backs that rested upon the foundation of their cousin, the Leader. They said to Ahmed, "We are the ones who appointed you a judge, so judge according to our orders" He replied, "And the law?" They said, "Leave it aside, we are the law." Ahmed could not imagine ignoring laws and article numbers, all of which he had learned by heart and all of which had seeped into his blood and throbbed in the heart of his convictions. Therefore he hesitated.

They sent to his house a woman carrying a briefcase. She opened it near the tea glasses on the table and brought out bundles of banknotes, pretending she needed his help in a case. Disturbed but resolute, Ahmed dumped the bundles back into the case, so they snapped his picture. They invaded his house and threw him in jail for graft. His children returned to my aunt, who was busy weeping and wiping away the thread of blood trickling down from Ijayel's Adam's apple.

The price of the bullets was paid. Qasim was buried near Abdul-Wahid, as my aunt wished. She sat between her two graves every morning, crying and laughing and arranging the white pebbles on the two mounds, kissing the two grave markers and scolding the boys for their early departure, then asking them about their health and whether the meeting with the ancestors had taken place yet. Then she told them news: "Your father is mute in bed. Warda did not remarry. Saadi left. They say he's doing well because he works for the government. Ahmed is in prison. Hasiba works in the fields and weeps. Shaima is sick and Ibrahim is busy singing. Mahmoud, I don't know. And Abood, apple of my eye, his nightly howl has gotten louder since you . . . in the village square . . . Qasim."

Abood's voice now scared the children, and when they heard his howling, even women and the elderly shivered because it was loud and agonizing, as if he were a hungry wolf. "The apple of his mother's eye." Some people complained about him, so Warda took him around to the doctors but they could not silence him. Then, accompanied by my aunt, she dragged him to dervishes, who advised them to dig a hole similar to a grave near the two graves of his brothers for him to sleep in and to cover it at night with a wooden door.

Many of the villagers, enthusiastic about the dervishes' advice, helped in the digging and the making of the door. At each sunset, after feeding him his dinner, Warda took him there. She lowered him into the hole and then closed the door over him. On the door she placed a few rocks so the dogs could not lift it. In the morning my aunt brought him back with her after the feast of tears between her two graves . . . her three graves.

Warda became more withdrawn and

distracted. She looked inside herself for the troop of absentees and their final departure, always mindful of the fact that she had not finished her talk with Qasim—that interrupted talk, the only talk she ever had with him or anyone else about something other than the practical and the routine. She contemplated her father, who became more resigned and withdrawn. He grew emaciated and wan, wasting away by the minute. Like ice he melted, and when she saw him close-up in his bed, he looked small, as if she were seeing him from afar.

She entered the guestroom, returning from the baking oven with a plate of warm bread on her head. She found his eyes fixed on the painting. Two eyes and a thread of blood. She looked at him, then at the picture. She stood between them, shifting her eyes from one to the other. She took the plate off her head and set it on the floor, then broke off a crust of burnt bread. She looked at her father looking at the painting, then moved toward it. It was up high, so she put two pillows under her feet and raised herself on her toes. With the edge of the burnt bread she drew a black arrow that pierced the center of the green heart and the red homeland's heart. She drew the arrow with an agonized violence, exactly as had that youth who had come with the pest-control teams of the Ministry of Social Welfare at the beginning of a far-off summer. She remembered how he had looked at her and then painted that white poison arrow that killed her mother's cow. Now her arrow was black from the char of burnt bread.

When she put its thin edge on the painting, she heard behind her the cry of her father: "Yes, yes, Qasim, I understand!" She turned around and saw him pointing at the painting, raising his head as if he wanted to get up. She ran to help him, but he motioned for her to leave. She settled his head on the pillow until he was comfortable, the sign of which was the hint of a smile on the aged, emaciated lips sunken in the thicket of his hoary beard and mustache. After that his silence became more constant, along with the bleeding of his needle and his gradual maceration, day after day, until he withered in his bed and died. When they carried him to rest near the graves of his sons, he was light , like a dead turtledove.

9

The war, as Ismael had predicted, finally came to an end. Despite his accustomed mendacity, for once he had told the truth. Mahmoud left the country, sneaking off through the North. Abood disappeared from his hole one night, no one knew where to or even how. His nocturnal howl stopped forever. In the morning my aunt looked into his hole tens of times—hundreds. There was no howling in it. She questioned Ijayel, Qasim, and Abdul-Wahid, next to whom Abood had been lying, but they told her nothing, so she cried. My aunt wept until the blue water of her cataract-dimmed eyes trembled. Warda wanted to howl for her in his stead, but she was drowning in her absent-mindedness and lacerating sorrow and did not even pay attention to the rising star of her brother Saadi, who after the war started appearing on TV at the head of the League of the Leader's Beloved, carrying the scissors to cut the ribbons at the openings of his "gift galleries," where he displayed the presents he often received. A snapshot: Saadi in the midst of applause, kissing the children that carried the flowers to welcome him, covering his head with the headcord and the *kaffiyya,* and on his face that oafish smile and dead features.

The seasons of the year do not mean anything to him, to us, to anybody, to Warda or my aunt. For the changes are not that the sky is rainy or sunny. The changes are here—point to your hearts and draw a circle around yourselves to include the others.

Hasiba was mired in the mud of her field's irrigation ditches, baring her arm to the changes of the seasons until it lost its whiteness. For whom should it remain white, snow-white, now that Qasim had gone? My aunt continued to visit her four graves every day, and Warda accompanied her every Thursday to cry with her sometimes and to drift in her absent-mindedness at other times. With pebbles my aunt outlined a triangle next to the graves and said, "This is my grave." She looked at Warda as if to give her strength of will, or so that she too might indicate that her own grave would be next to theirs, but Warda did not budge. She did not love death.

And although she, like the rest, did not know to where or how Abood had disappeared, she wished that her own death when its time came would be a disappearance—to where she did not know, but she did not want a burial.

My aunt delicately wiped off the foot of Ijayel's grave marker as if she were once more wiping away the blood thread trickling down his Adam's apple. She said to Warda, or to herself, "I rarely asked him anything, but I do remember asking him the meaning of the word 'nails' that his mother repeated three times before she breathed her final breath. He said, 'She meant life, like the silliness of her clan's gatherings at night when they used to heat nails in fire until they reddened, then drop them in a bowl of cold water so they produced a sound, "Kishhhhh," the sound of the cooling of a red-hot nail. "Kishhhhh." Laughter. They laughed for that "Kishhhhh."' * 'Nails, nails, nails.'—his mother said it three times and died. I wish I could say that and die."

---

*See the novel *Da Ba Da* by Hasan Mitlak. p. 220.

After that my aunt spoke to her absent ones, relating the news, scolding them for leaving, and teasing Abood's empty hole. She reminded him of his beauty as a baby and his childhood smile, then went back to her weeping and wailed:

> It crossed borders and passed
> My life and slipped away,
> And all for which we labored
> Is rushing water gone astray.

Ismael, passing on the path near the cemetery, overheard her lament. His feet scraped the pebbles and raised dust. He stopped to allow the dust of his feet to rise to his face and noticed my aunt's grief. He wished he had carried his rebec with him to put her sorrows into music and to bewail his own sorrows along with her—orphanhood, loneliness, loss, poverty, and mendacity.

His father used to prophesy, and everything he prophesied happened. He was only ever wrong once, and that was in predicting Judgment Day, for he died and it did not come. Less of a seer than his father, Ismael nonetheless predicted the end of the war, and so it ended.

Before that he predicted the flood, Abbas's wedding, Qasim's death, Mahmoud's departure, and Saadi's arrival.

Ismael described the present period as "the era of Saadi's friends and the hookers." He expected another war. Through the dust he saw Warda, head hanging, by the edge of Abood's hole. He stepped out of the dust and approached until he stood by the empty grave. Going unnoticed, he squatted on the edge of the hole in front of my aunt and, even without his rebec, replied to her elegy with one of his own:

> Sorrow, ache, and parting,
> > Separation and the world:
> O my soul, woe is on you,
> > Surprised that you could hold!

Warda wailed at the sound of his voice, and my aunt's weeping intensified upon hearing his words. She rejoined:

> Here's an hour, here's a year,
> > Here's my whole life rent.
> Wound upon wound, O soul,
> > Which one do I mend?

Warda cried, my aunt felt a great release, and Ismael answered her in the same tempo of sorrow:

> Wishing to see the dead,
> My soul is mad, distraught.
> The earth slammed shut on him—
> I go longing to see naught.

My aunt moaned, ignoring the pain in her eyes. Warda's weeping grew louder. Ismael burst out in a cry, so my aunt responded to this rite of mourning, adding:

> Allah, to you I cry
> From this bleeding wound.
> Come, heal it quickly,
> Or bring this soul to swoon!

They cried until they emptied their eyes, yet their hearts did not empty. Then they calmed down and wiped the drops from their reddened noses. The silence of the graves overwhelmed them, and so Ismael felt that he had to say something. He said, without caring that what he was saying was a prophecy he did not really foresee,

"Rest assured, you're going to find Abood. You'll find him, or he'll come back, and so will Mahmoud." Those were not the words he had wanted to say. He also knew that the two women did not believe him because Warda did not raise her head and my aunt went on wiping her nose with the edge of her black cloak, so he added, "Rest assured, I will take revenge on those who hurt you, those who hurt us all."

Warda looked at him sharply, as if she were discovering his existence at that instant, as if she were getting to know him for the first time, a man other than that rebec player stigmatized by his mendacity, not Ismael the lonely and poor who lived in his father's mud hut on the outskirts of the village. He responded to Warda with a grave look, saying, "I have a plan. A hellish one."

Warda gazed at him questioningly. After she finished drying her face and without hearing what he had said, my aunt asked him, "Who washes your clothes for you, Ismael?" Then she added, "Allah help you, how do you get by, my son?" Turning his face from Warda and letting out a deep breath as he rose, he answered her, "Like a crow, aunt."

He left them, followed by Warda's eyes until he reached the pebble road and the dust. She got up hurriedly and screamed at him, "Ismael, stop!" He halted and she ran to ask him, "Do you mean that you'll avenge us on that distant stranger?"

He replied, "That very one."

She asked, "The one who killed Qasim and Abdul-Wahid and Fauzi and my father and ...?"

He interrupted her. "I've never hated anyone the way I hate him."

She said, "Neither have I."

He said, "I'll smash him into crumbs the way he smashed us."

She asked, "You're going to tell me the plan?"

He answered, "I will tell you the plan. You alone, because the others laugh."

She asked, "Are you sincere in your hatred of him?"

He answered, "As sincere as the tears we shed now."

She asked, "Do you dream of getting rid of him?"

He answered, "More than I dream of getting rid of poverty."

Warda gazed deeply into his eyes and said, "You are a man worthy of respect." He was abashed before her gaze as he beheld the beauty rekindle in her face and cast off its haggardness. He added, "But I'm . . . but I'm busy with the plan."

She asked, "Will you marry me?"

He was nonplussed by the total incandescence of her face and affirmed with joyful determination, "I will carry out the plan."

Warda called to my aunt that now they should go back home.

10

Warda married Ismael and promised to bear him only sons, and he promised her to name all of them "Qasim." My aunt did not object, Ahmed did not object, but all the villagers tittered into their fingers, then carried their laughter to Saadi in the capital, so he came to reproach her for marrying Ismael. Saadi said, "He's a liar, and he used to run away during the war." She looked at him in silence. He added, "You must leave him. He does not suit my position as head of the League of the Leader's Beloved. What would they say about me if they knew that my brother-in-law is a liar who does nothing but play the rebec?" She said, "But he's a man worthy of respect." He screamed, "What for?" She said, "We have the same dream." He said, "You're nuts!"

Saadi wanted to talk more with her but did not know what to say or how to say it, so he mumbled, then said resolutely, "He's . . . he's not nice." Then he went to Hasiba, hoping that she would help him persuade Warda because he did not speak well. She was out but her son was home, so he convinced Ibrahim to go with him to the capital to sing there and become a famous singer like all the poets who sang for the Leader. Ibrahim was happy to go, but Hasiba, when she came back from the fields, jumped on him and pummeled him with her sunburnt fists. "You want to sing to the murderer of your father, you son of . . . son of Hasiba?"

She kicked him all the way to his room, locked the door, and then turned to Saadi, who moved closer to her, drawn by her rage and rough temper. "Calm down, Hasiba," Saadi said. "Calm down, for even you have to think of yourself." He touched her arm with desire in his eyes. She was infuriated yet uncertain of how to react. She spat in his face, and he realized the danger in what he had done. He hurried to leave, but Hasiba was quick enough to throw her shoe, which hit the corner of his head before he disappeared outside the door and from the village forever. But he still peeked out from the TV, and she still spat and threw her shoe at him whenever he appeared with the Leader, who threatened to fight the whole world in defense of "sovereignty, pride, and honor."

Ismael swore before Warda that he would not take part in the new war and that he was determined to keep busy with his plan. Every day he showed Warda new details and modifications, so she demanded that he include among his revisions punishment for singers and poets, something of which she never would have thought of before Hasiba told her about Saadi's attempt to influence Ibrahim. He promised her to add that later, and Warda proceeded to forward his promise to Hasiba. When Warda entered Hasiba's house and saw the door to Qasim's painting room shut, she voiced her desire to have all the pictures that he had done of her since childhood. Hasiba opened the painting room door for her and, after stopping by the house of her bed-ridden daughter Shaima, who looked yellow and haggard like an old thread of wool, went out to the fields. As usual, she did not return until after sunset, after exhausting her body with work as though she were taming it.

Darkness prevailed over the universe, and then a moon illumined it, a moon that Hasiba gravely contemplated but could find no meaning in. It was ordinary, bare like a grim piece of metal. There was nothing in it, not even Qasim's face. The cemetery and the fields were dark, though some scattered lights pierced the darkness of the village. In times like this she, like the rest, used to hear the sad tunes of Ismael's rebec. But he quit playing after marrying Warda and left the space of the village, fields, cemetery, and the entire world to the croaking of frogs, chirping of grasshoppers, howling of jackals, barking of dogs, and shouting of boys playing in between the haystacks, all drowned out, from time to time, by the braying of a donkey.

Darkness. Muddied feet. Distant stars. Meaningless moon. Dreamless head. Aimless fortitude. And a warmth that was sad . . . very sad. Watch out for the blue water in your eyes, Aunt, for it has increased. You will be blinded by it, just as Warda will be killed by her desire for salvation or life or revenge or defiance . . . What defiance! She does not like death. She is insistent on survival, leaving in her wake Wardas and Qasims, heedless of the village's loss of the tunes of Ismael's rebec. Those in the village used to have their dinner while he slept hungry, using his rebec for a pillow. Now he has had his dinner, and here he is, hovering like a butterfly around a flower, Warda. Carnations perfumed her armpits and her face glistened with that dream. Coyly she swayed her bare shoulders. Beautiful . . . beautiful . . ."How beautiful!"

Ismael could not resist the charm of her smile, which tormented him every night with its provisional refusal until he repeated the details of his plan and its new revisions. After that she would give herself to him unconditionally. More than anyone else he had ever known, she had no limits. He asked himself, "Did Fauzi and Aqiel realize that?"

Warda was an infinite creature. There was no end to her, but she needed a beginning—some beginning, even if a dream or a lie. He reached out to her, so she gathered in her shoulders and coiled in refusal, saying, "The plan." She lay on the straw mat. Ismael lay beside her, half on the mat and half on her. Once again he told her of his plan, and then she helped him lift his other half over her. He trembled in elation, dancing with her long locks spread beneath them. The hair swayed him, or perhaps he swayed the hair. And Warda was hair and eyes and cheeks and lips and shoulders and heart and . . . Warda was endless, and the absent were not absent to her. That distant stranger, the intruder: "He has made us into scattered crumbs." Ismael answered her, "I will make him into scattered crumbs." His panting quickened, their panting quickened, as she asked him intermittently, "And the po . . . And the poets?" He crumbled over her, "I will ma . . ke . . . the . . m . . . in . . . to . . . s . c . . a . . t . . t . . e . . r . . e . . d . . . c . . r . . u . . m . . b . . s." She repeated with him in the ecstasy of endlessness and the incessant dream, "Sc . . a . . t . . t . . e . . r . . e . . d . . . cr . . u . . m . . b . . s . . ."

Empty Handed

Perhaps "Empty Handed" is another attempt to repeat what I tried to describe in my story "The Jackal's Wedding"—when rain falls while the sun is out. Estrangement bereft of its meaning. Disconnected existence. Exile in the Babylonian sense, temporal more than spatial. It is the detention of the present whose prolongation burns us. I do not know what to call my intention to search for Mahmoud while in reality I do not search for him. I wake up in the afternoon. I rummage through the newspapers before I wash my face, then discard them in disappointment. "Nothing new about the homeland." A shower, coffee with milk, then a cigarette and a look around from the balcony. "Nothing new in exile." I resort again, perhaps for the thousandth time, to reading the only two letters that have arrived since my departure.

Days that are all the same, years that efface my dreams and commingle with memory in an embittered exhaustion. I pace through the streets, looking at peoples' necks. Am I the only one who feels the pinch of the hedgehog's needle in his throat? I almost ask the passersby, "Do you see a thread of blood trickling down the apple that I inherited from Adam?"

We, the scattered in space, did not choose our present locations but arrived at them because of the gas explosions in the eternal fire chambers. And those who sputter in suffocation do not look at the ground where their feet tread. We did not choose our new lands, we who were kicked out from our old one when it was crushed mercilessly. This is why we endure our agonies, akin to being flayed alive. The ones who preceded us still turn on the valve of their memories in conversation, asking about Azzawi's café and the statue of the Winged Bull and Basra's dried lemons. The ones who followed later are nauseated by all this complaining, so they keep it brief: "Safe is he who has entered his grave."

Here in the streets of Granada, we weep with the Palestinians. We cry like women over homelands that we did not know how to preserve like men. How often have we spat at our mustaches before the mirrors of the West and then ended up shaving them off? We are no good except for blackening pages with sorrowful cries. I wonder if paper-recycling companies can supply enough sheets for the flood of stories about my homeland.

I flutter back and forth, a stranger here, between the fleshwounds and the depth's lacerations, the bitterness of evanescence and the waiting masked in no waiting, patience and nothingness, tasting and dying, surrounded by the Spaniards: prattle and prattle and dogs and smoke and advertising pages, beautiful statues that do not understand what happened there to my aunt and her children. Vacancy, dancing, always the flow of frigid kisses despite the hasty blowing of their ashes, beauty sticky with fluff. For all this I drag myself to the café and the dance floor, the gardens and the metro. I live torn between exile and my country, pained by the sight of a laughing man and enraptured by a woman of fashion.

I disembark from the circular metro number 6 after riding its circle. Subterranean circles whose number I do not fathom. At the corner of the staircase leans a woman enfeebled by addiction. She lowers her pants, squats, and urinates. At the glass of the gate stands a black youth with silver earrings handing out flyers for a strip bar to the passersby. Saturday night has fallen on its dizzy creatures. The street clock points to two. I stroll into the first bar, sit in the farthest corner, and drift away, gazing into the darkness . . .

> "But it's the earth,
> The perfect porcelain pasture
> —The Scattered Crumbs.
> I'm a brass anklet,
> Beneath brass earrings.
> I'm the name of the perfect woman,

And the body of the perfect woman,
And the fabric . . . all translucent.
People around me distant,
Dark is my hand.

It's the earth
And the sight that seduces insight to gape,
To cull the bitter and the static, dark in soul.
It's the earth,
And this dark window
Bleeds dark sweat,
A pasture darker to me than what I know.

Running are the porcelain trees,
And I hide from the roar of their onslaught,
From their needles' screams.

It's the earth,
And the coffee,
And the Scattered Crumbs."*

*The poem is by the poet Mahir al-Asfar.